ABIGAIL STEWART

SELECT SCREEN

WHISKEY TIT

NYC & VT

Edited by Brad Casenave.

Published in the United States and Canada by Whisk(e)y Tit: www.whiskeytit.com. If you wish to use or reproduce all or part of this book for any means, please let the author and publisher know. You're pretty much required to, legally.

ISBN 978-1-952600-59-3

“Perfect people aren't real, and real people aren't perfect.”
— Paulo Coelho via Twitter

“I don't think Snape has ever said anything untrue, or anything that did not happen or was false, not about anyone. I don't have any doubt about it.”
— Chamber of Secrets, a Harry Potter Discussion Board

“But everything falls away, try as you might to stop it. And for whatever returns to you, be grateful.”
— Rachel Cusk, *Outline*

1

Chuck woke up from a fitful sleep. He'd had the same dream again, the one where he was playing a first-person shooter, but for real. The dream always started *in medias res* and he looked down at his hands holding a starter weapon at the spawn point. He recognized his placement on the game map he'd committed to memory. Moments after entering the dreamscape, his back was pressed up against the imaginary city's interior stone wall, he could feel the uneven surface through his shirt. Why didn't he have any tactical gear on? He needed to find some.

It was always empty, the city, no civilians, vacant shopping stalls. No one had taken any of the items left behind in haste by invisible inhabitants — carts overfilled with sun-ripened fruit, bags of colorful spices that thickened the air, live chickens scratching in their cages — it all spilled over like a cornucopia into the battle's backdrop.

Chuck surged forward, across the sandy courtyard littered with boxes and sandbags and places designed to hide behind. His eyesight blurred in the direct light of the midday sun, lens flares filled his vision and he pointed his gun toward the top of the walls, blindly searching for snipers. He moved quickly now, and having reached the opposite side, he took a moment to look back and caught an enemy emerging from the spawn point. Two taps — headshot. The body fell to the ground in silence — if a body falls in a video game and no one hears it, does it matter? Chuck knew he had to move before someone else determined where the shot had come from.

A tactical chest appeared only a few feet away and he opened it — bullets and a gun upgrade, no vest. He loaded the new weapon, a lighter and more accurate model. He didn't need to work so hard to steady it, it could autofocus on a target.

Chuck felt sweat drip down his shoulders and pool at his lower back. It was so hot and the sand had begun to stick to him. Focus, he needed to focus. He thought he saw a black muzzle flash in his periphery. He took a deep breath and turned the corner; he was face to face with the enemy now. Chuck drew his knife and stabbed him several times, the knife entered flesh without resistance — a silent kill, he was safe for the moment.

Chuck kept his body crouched toward the ground like a primordial creature just emerged from the sand. Everything around him was illuminated by the too-bright sun; harsh shadows challenged reality with midday phantoms. In the distance, shots rang out — the vibrating blast of a grenade nearly knocked him over, but he steadied himself. He crouched into a squat to check his weapons. His hands moved quickly through the inventory, muscle memory. It was then he saw a man strolling through the empty sandstone hall in front of him, he moved so slowly he may as well have been whistling to himself, only Chuck couldn't tell as he had a scarf wrapped loosely around his face. The entire square stood still; the gunfire stopped. *Why wasn't he crouched down? He must be new*, Chuck thought.

The man wore the same assigned colors as Chuck's team, so Chuck lowered his weapon and raised a hand in greeting. In response, the man fired two shots into Chuck's chest. Brrat, tat — friendly fire. Even in the dream, Chuck felt the pain, white hot like the scalding sun he could no longer shield from his eyes. The man leaned over his fallen body and began to unravel the scarf that would inevitably reveal his face, but it was always then that Chuck woke up.

If numbChux has a million fans, I'm one of them.
If numbChux has five fans, I'm one of them.
If numbChux has one fan, that one is me.
If numbChux has no fans, I'm no longer alive.
If the world is against numbChux, I'm against the world.

UrGod @YourMomsMessiah: I hate to say it, but my man numbChux is washed up

BJ @bjsrcool_ replying to @YourMomsMessiah: *he may not be clean but he ain't washed*

It's Randy @duhrandy replying to @YourMomsMessiah: *get outta here with this bandwagon shit*

Toad @princetoadstool replying to @YourMomsMessiah and @bjsarecool: *get Chux some dryer sheets and send him home*

Cedric pulled the blankets over his head and concealed himself inside a makeshift cave of fabric, muffling the plaintive voice of his mother from outside his bedroom door. The screen in his hand filled the false grotto with a pervasive blue glow, a campfire gone cold.

"Cedric, I'm going to be late for work! We need to leave in twenty minutes."

The boy gripped his tablet and shouted back, "I'm *not* going!"

He heard Ellen, his mother, frustratedly grappling with the unforgiving metal lock, then a loud crash as she fell forward into the room. She dodged the detritus he'd strewn across the floor in an effort to further impede her.

"You're not allowed to lock your door, you know that."

Her voice was subdued now, the most insurmountable obstacle overcome. She plunged her hands into the bedclothes and grabbed at him. Her arms contorted like pale, flesh-colored snakes in the otherworldly light and Cedric retreated further back into the corner of his bed.

"I'm not going! I'm not going!"

Ellen ripped the covers off and exposed her son to the world once more, an unformed caterpillar ripped too early from his cocoon. She watched his eyes narrow to slits.

"You have ten minutes to get ready. Give me that."

The scowl on her twelve-year old's face almost gave Ellen pause, he looked at her as though she had betrayed him in some unforgivable way. Then, she thought again of her boss, his distinct lack of compassion for tardiness, and snatched the device from Cedric's hands. She thought for a moment that he might cry and felt embarrassed for them both, but he sniffed once and wiped his nose with the arm of his pajamas.

"Ten minutes," she repeated.

She waited in the kitchen, her heart beating rapidly after their exchange, privately worrying he might not come down at all. What would she do then? She put the tablet in a kitchen drawer, on top of an old copy of *Parenting* magazine, knowing she had no further means to compel him.

Ellen opened the fridge, then closed it again. She put a piece of toast in the toaster and counted the number of seconds before it popped up. She spread a thick layer of peanut butter over the top and set it on a scuffed, grey plate. She poured a glass of milk and set the breakfast pairing on the kitchen counter where Cedric usually sat at a barstool and ate each morning. These were the little routines she normally enjoyed, the times she felt closest to her son.

Cedric finally emerged from his dungeon still wearing a fearsome scowl that Ellen now realized reminded her of his father, she banished the thought. He was wearing pants she knew he'd fished out of the laundry hamper and she worried the pants might smell, but couldn't risk compromising their tentative truce.

"Eat your toast."

He took a petulant bite, made a face, and replaced the toast. He drank half the glass of milk, then shot her a challenging glance as if to say, 'Well?'

"Alright, let's go."

Silence permeated the car ride and Ellen turned on the smooth jazz station to fill this new space between them. She parked near the front of the school, but not directly in the car lane with the other mothers. Cedric hated when she made a show of dropping him off.

"Have a good day." Her goodbye was cut short by the car door's slam.

Once her son was safely inside the doors of his middle school, she switched the radio to Rock Classics 101 and blared Def Leppard as she sped down the highway toward her office.

Her boss greeted her by looking first at his watch, then nodding approval. Ellen rushed to her cubicle and logged in, she did a quick once over of Slack and her email to verify there were no emergencies before heading to the break room for a coffee. Several colleagues were gathered around the coffee machine clutching their mugs as the ancient thing sputtered out another dark potful.

"Hi Ellen."

"You look tired, rough morning?"

Ellen smoothed her hair and fixed a smile on her face, "Just need some caffeine."

"Don't we all!"

General laughter ensued, then faded into bland conversation wondering how it could possibly be Wednesday already.

Ellen poured herself a cup of coffee and walked back to her cubicle, basking in the silence. She hated making small talk almost as much as she hated the office. The fluorescent lighting refracted off her screen in a bright array that left her blinking away black spots. As her mind wandered, she considered, not for the first time, Cedric's resemblance to his father.

She best remembered Tommy standing down by the creek tossing flat stones that skimmed the water with a grace that seemed detached from his imposing physical appearance. His broad shoulders were backlit by the afternoon sun and she watched his hands, rough and red from working on the line at a local diner, toss stone after stone with no sign of tiring. He made the smallest movement a dance and Ellen found her inner self shouting *Encore!*

Tommy kept himself apart from their group and it was easy for her to romanticize the deep and introspective thoughts he surely had staring out at the running creek. Now, she wondered if he was thinking about anything at all.

One afternoon, while they all drank cheap beer and worked on their suntans in the back of Chad's pickup, Ellen lost the thread of her friends' conversation in her search for the outline of Tommy's body by the creek's edge. Without him, the afternoon felt incomplete, like a puzzle missing a single corner piece. She left the protective circle of three girlfriends' laughter and picked her way down to the edge of the creek, along the pebble beach, to finally stick her toes in the water next to Tommy.

Neither of them said anything at first, then Ellen picked up a stone with her toes and lifted it to her hand. He did not comment on her dexterity. She flung the rock across the water and watched as it sank unceremoniously into the murky creek. This time, he laughed.

"Here, you have to hold your arm level and kind of flick it forward." He tossed another rock and Ellen watched it skip until the opposite shore of the creek halted its progress. She thought for a moment it might skip right into the woods on the other side and disappear.

They stood, side by side, skipping rocks until the sun began to set. Minnows nibbled at her toes and Ellen wiggled her feet only to watch them disperse, then return once more. Water bugs skimmed around her bare legs in practiced pirouettes and, next to her, Tommy mechanically raised his arm to release another rock, then another. Ellen went back to the truck and returned with two beers. They stood in the creek and drank them in silence, listening to the doves call to one another from their secret places in the thick grove of trees.

At the end of that day, once darkness fell around them and their friends had started a campfire ringed with rocks at the creek's edge, Tommy kissed her.

They spent one brilliant summer wrapped up in the assuredness of youth and the golden embrace of the sun. They lay entwined in the hammock on Tommy's property for hours doing nothing, saying nothing. Ellen's long legs burnished gold as the days went on and Tommy grew a fuzzy blonde beard.

"What are you thinking about?"

"Nothing."

Ellen laughed, "You can't always be thinking about nothing."

"Well, I am."

Then, they'd revert to silence again until Ellen asked another question or mentioned they go somewhere together.

"Why don't we ever go out? Are you embarrassed of me?" she pressed. She kept her voice light, to show it was only a joke.

"I thought I'd found someone who understood me."

His accusation and small, hurt eyes always silenced her. But even though they never said much of anything, at the end of that summer, Ellen told him she was pregnant.

Tommy's response was a simple nod, then a phone call to his friend who had offered him a job he hadn't mentioned to Ellen.

Tommy got a job as a line cook at one of the nicer pubs in town and they moved into a studio apartment together. Ellen set up a crib at the foot of their bed and kept her teller position at the bank. She worked the bank's drive-through window and was able to spend most of the day off her feet, counting cash and listening to the adult contemporary music piped through the speakers. It felt peaceful. She brought in one of the sonogram printouts and pinned it above her workspace. She waved to the kids in the back of the cars, amused by their bored looks. She slipped them lollipops via the pneumatic tube return and watched their look of wonder at receiving a treat as though by magic. She imagined herself in place of the mothers and rubbed her belly as she counted out stacks of twenties, tens, fives, and ones.

Cedric was a quiet baby and Ellen really thought he was the most adorable in the nursery when they first went to see him. She didn't say anything but stood with Tommy at the window. He hung back and peered over her shoulder into the beds.

"Is he that one?"

"Yeah. He's perfect," she sighed.

Tommy didn't respond.

He put in longer hours at the restaurant, hoping to make himself indispensable. In the end, he did. The owner offered him an opportunity to work at his new restaurant in Anchorage; Tommy said yes without much of a backward glance, and Ellen was still here.

"Hey, Ellen!"

The high-pitched voice cut through her daydream and drew her back to reality where her coffee had gone cold and her computer screen had switched over to a screen saver of the desert.

Behind her, the receptionist stared quizzically before explaining, "You've got a phone call." Ellen detected a hint of something, pity perhaps, in the woman's lowered voice, but she walked away and gave Ellen space to answer her ancient desk phone.

"Hello?"

"Is this Miss Turlock?"

"Speaking."

"Your son, Cedric, has been a part of an incident and needs to be picked up."

"Oh god, is he okay?"

"He's fine."

"What happened?"

"I'd prefer if we spoke about it in person."

"Can we do that after school? I am working."

"I'm afraid not."

Ellen looked at the computer clock. It was almost noon.

"Okay, if I leave now I can come get him on my lunch break."

"I would appreciate it."

She hung up the phone; the receiver landed a little too hard in the cradle and her cubicle neighbor stopped speaking for a moment to eavesdrop.

Ellen grabbed her bag, walked toward the lobby without making eye contact, then drove herself to her son's school. The rock station drowned out her confused inner monologue of anger and fear.

The principal met her in the office and they shook hands. Ellen tried to remember if she'd ever met this man before, maybe at an open house or back-to-school night. Something about his button-down shirt with a tie and jeans, his attempt to be professional yet trendy, made her immediately dislike him.

"I'd like to speak with you for a moment before we bring Cedric in."

"Okay."

"Cedric and a couple of other boys were involved in a fight today."

"Oh," Ellen wasn't sure how to respond. Her mind reeled; Cedric had never expressed any physical inclination toward violence before. Was this her fault for taking the tablet? Or not listening when he said he didn't want to go to school?

"He's fine, the other boys are too, but it appears they were fighting about some sort of video game or online video. I'm not sure, to be honest. The thing is, once we separated them on the playground, Cedric picked up a rock and threw it directly at another kid. Unfortunately, a teacher had stepped in between them, and it hit her in the arm."

Tommy skipping rocks flashed before Ellen's eyes.

"It drew blood. The teacher doesn't want to push for any sort of disciplinary or legal action."

Ellen let out the breath she had been holding.

"But, according to our school handbook, Cedric will be suspended for three days."

"I understand. What about the other boys?"

"They are each getting one day of suspension. Is it okay if we bring Cedric in now?"

Ellen nodded and turned toward the door to face her son, who entered the room like a broken prisoner, arms folded and clasping his backpack in front of him like a protective shield. He took a seat next to her and Ellen thought how small he seemed in the adult-sized chair, his feet barely touching the floor.

"Cedric, I want to hear in your own words what happened this afternoon," the principal began.

The boy squirmed and didn't answer.

"Cedric," Ellen said warningly.

"They were teasing me. I just fought back."

"About what?"

"They were saying that numbChux is dead."

The principal and Ellen exchanged a glance.

"Nunchucks?"

"NumbChux, with an X."

"Okay, who is that?"

"He's this streamer for the game we all play, *Trash Fighters*. Only I am a numbChux fan and all those guys like PorkyDig. They kept saying numbChux is washed and

Porky is gonna win the next tournament, the big one in Las Vegas. They said Chux hasn't posted in weeks because he's dead and they started making fun of me saying only betas like Chux. They kept calling me 'betaChux.'"

Cedric lapsed into silence and Ellen tried to untangle what her son was talking about. She knew he watched *Trash Fighters* on Twitch and felt like the name numbChux had been mentioned before, but none of it seemed worthy of a fight and three days suspension.

"I think your physical response was inappropriate, Cedric," she finally said.

"They tripped me first!" He turned to her for the first time, and she saw his red eyes, that he'd been crying, and a bruise near his chin. Her heart contracted, but she continued.

"The principal says you're going to need to stay home for three days as punishment. And that means no TV and no video games. You will work on your school assignments and read for English class, is that clear?"

Cedric nodded and the principal seemed satisfied; he nodded in tandem with an implicit approval of her parenting skills.

"Now, let's go. I need to take you home."

She shook hands again with the principal and marched her son out to the car.

Once they were both safely seat-belted in, Ellen pressed her foot down on the gas pedal and they flew down the streets toward home. She drove recklessly and her son's eyes stayed wide, focused on the road. They didn't say anything, but the classic rock station played Aerosmith in the background. She pulled up in front of their small duplex and took a deep breath.

"Do you have the key?"

He nodded.

"Go inside, and I swear if you touch the television, I will know. Do not make me angrier than I already am, Cedric. We will discuss all of this when I get home."

She watched her son retreat inside, his backpack still just a little wider than his shoulders. She half expected him to turn around and wave like he always did when he was a smaller child and she left him with the babysitter, but he didn't even look back. She flipped a U-turn and sped back to work, arriving with just a minute to spare. Ellen felt, for once, thankful that they lived in such a small town.

The receptionist brought her a couple of phone memos on pink squares of paper and stood in the doorway of Ellen's cubicle after handing them over, waiting for an explanation, an outburst, anything she could take back to the other girls as gossip.

"Thanks Mindy," Ellen called over her shoulder. She wouldn't give her the satisfaction of weaponized office comradery.

Tommy, that fucker, was probably still in Alaska. The earlier golden haze she'd cast around their summer together turned to ash. *A side effect of climate change*, she thought. Ellen knew he'd started working on a fishing boat shortly after he left. No one ever told her what happened with the restaurant. Chad acted cagey when she asked him directly. Tommy sent her a postcard that said, "It's cold here. Thinking about you and C." And another with a picture of the marina where his boat was docked that said even more simply, "Going out tomorrow!" After that, she didn't hear much, but received sporadic checks, until those dried up as well.

"You should go after him for child support," her friends advised.

But she couldn't do it. Part of her didn't want to sully what they had; another part wanted to prove she could do it alone. Although Cedric had never asked about his father, the absence felt conspicuous, particularly on a day like today.

Ellen logged back into her computer and tended to her clients' needs, returned the necessary phone calls, and walked to the kitchen for another cup of coffee. She poured vanilla creamer in and watched it swirl delicately in the muddy darkness of her mug.

Back at her desk, she opened Google and typed 'Numb Chuck' into the search bar. *Did you mean numbChux*, it asked. She clicked 'yes.' Her screen immediately flooded with articles, videos, and social media posts for 'numbChux,' often accompanied by *Trash Fighters* tournaments all over North America, Europe and Japan. In one photo, the man known as Chux held aloft a trophy and wore what resembled a soccer jersey, only with a graphics card brand and energy drink logo adorning it.

A few cursory minutes of research revealed he was a streamer of some renown and a competitive gamer who had recently gone missing. At least he'd stopped streaming and posting his twice weekly YouTube videos. His Twitter had similarly gone dark. In turn, Chux's fans, whose ages seemed to range from eleven to forty, were bereft and creating post after post in online forums, filling the YouTube comment sections with conspiracies, and warring with one another on social media.

Ellen realized how disconnected she was from the world her son inhabited, this online world that had spilled over into the schoolyard. Her middle-class life and cubicle job kept her at arm's length from people who made thousands of dollars playing video games competitively or spent twelve hours a day filming themselves playing said games. One video titled: "The Ultimate *Trash Fighters* Tier List" ranked numbChux as the number one player, another listed him at number four. The comments underneath were filled with dissenting opinions and people posting line after line of nothing but woodchuck emojis, which was apparently how they showed their Chux support.

Chux was often described as 'wholesome' and 'based' and his young male followers felt betrayed by his absence. Some of them even referred to him as 'daddy' and wondered what they should do without his daily guidance, the routine he provided.

> »   What do we do without Daddy?
>   @numbChux where are you?

The raw obsession that pivoted to depression or anger in just a few days made Ellen uncomfortable. These invisible fans all felt he owed them something, but who was he? Just another kid, she thought. To be needed so fervently by strangers must be an unsettling thing. It made immediate sense to her why this young man had chosen to disappear himself from the internet as best he could.

Her co-workers began to shuffle past in twos and threes and Ellen realized it was almost five o'clock. She packed up her things and prepared herself to face Cedric.

Cedric was drinking a glass of milk and doing his math homework when she walked in. She briefly imagined him as an older man, a glass of whiskey by his hand, resigned to an evening at home. He looked up when she walked in. The bruise on his face had darkened. Ellen sat down beside him at the kitchen table and took a sip from his glass of milk, pretending it was something stronger.

"How was the rest of your day?"

Cedric shrugged.

"I looked up numbChux at work."

He didn't respond.

"A lot of people have a lot of opinions about him and I was just thinking how that must be so hard, to carry all of those expectations on your shoulders all the time."

"He didn't say anything online and he posts all the time, but he didn't tell us anything."

"Is that what you're upset about?"

"I'm upset because he's just gone."

"Don't you think he deserves a break? A vacation?"

Cedric went quiet again.

"Everyone with a difficult job takes a vacation every once in a while. Remember when we went to the lake last summer? That was really nice for me because I got to relax and spend time with you. And it seems like his job can be very difficult. Think about all the things people say to him online, just like those boys you fought with today. And he might come back still, but if he doesn't, you should be prepared to move on. Don't count on the everlasting presence of someone you don't know."

"I did feel like I knew him, I felt like we were friends."

They both lapsed into silence and Ellen put her hand on her son's arm. She stood to pour herself another glass of milk and get an apple out of the fridge. She sliced it, put it on a plate, and sat it between them. They each took a slice and Ellen leaned over to help her son figure out a difficult arithmetic problem.

Cecilia shut the red, metal door to her classroom and turned the lock. The rectangular window that ran almost the length of the door was still covered with brown paper from an active shooter drill. The relief of concealment, of no longer being on display, flooded her as she slid her body down to the floor like a slowly melting popsicle. At least on the floor it was cool, the only cool space that existed in her un-air-conditioned classroom.

When she'd brought a complaint about the heat to the administrators during a meeting, her assistant principal told her, "Just open the windows,"

She explained that the windows had been painted and would no longer open, that the paint was also most likely lead-based and peeling off in flakes. After the meeting, an older teacher took her aside and warned her to keep it to herself, she didn't want to get a reputation as a complainer, did she?

Cecilia's solution was to install several fans around the room, fans that people had handed to her alongside their pity.

"You're doing God's work," her neighbor said, divesting herself of a too-large living room fan that now blew warm air into Cecilia's hair while she explained fractions to a group of restless pre-teens.

Though it was lunchtime, she didn't have any energy to eat. Yesterday, during lunch duty, a huge fight erupted over something on the internet that she didn't understand. One of her quietest students had bloodied the nose of another, much larger, boy. Cecilia stepped in and pulled them apart, their eyes still closed to reality, their tiny fists swinging wildly at phantoms.

No one had trained her in student teaching on how to detach angry boys from one another once they'd latched on. People always say never try to separate fighting cats, but human children were surely different. Still, she'd ripped one of her favorite cardigans in the fracas, a rock had hit her at some point, and all the while the gym teacher, presumably her on-duty partner, had merely looked on, sipping a Diet Coke.

Cecilia escorted all three of the boys to the principal's office, surprised by their meek compliance now that the moment of battle had passed.

"You're bleeding," the principal commented.

"Oh, yeah. I think it's from the rock."

She bit her lip against the impulsive admission, afraid for all three of the boys as the principal strode into the office and shut his door.

"Sometimes, you have to let them fight it out," the gym teacher said once she had returned to her post against the white concrete walls of the cafeteria. He wore windbreaker pants and a lanyard around his neck that held his classroom keys, they fell just above his protruding belly and jangled like a cat's bell when he walked down the hallways. After lunch, he'd enlist some of the older students to help him move the fold-up wood and metal tables, clearing space so students could hit each other with foam balls. The thwack of plastic-coated foam against the beige rubber floor echoed all the way back to Cecilia's classroom.

When none of the boys came back to her classroom after lunch, she spent the rest of the day holding back tears. She cried when she got frustrated and it embarrassed her.

Cecilia didn't want anything to do with fights, she just wanted to teach math. During student teacher training, her mentor teacher had encouraged her to "be friends with your students!" Which had seemed easy enough at the time. Of course, she'd also told Cecilia to make sure she wiped the dry erase board in an up and down motion rather than back and forth, "to alleviate jiggle, which can be distracting to young boys," so perhaps her advice shouldn't be heeded.

Maybe I'm just not good at being friendly, she thought. I have to keep Googling their jokes and insults and some of them I'd just rather not know. No one takes me seriously in the department, even though I have a Master's degree now. My parents are disappointed in me for not going into accounting and my students hate me and I can't get any of their parents to respond to my emails...

Cecilia knew she was spiraling, probably due to low blood sugar, so she rose from the ground and opened the top drawer of her desk, the one she kept locked and full of shelf-stable snacks. She ate a granola bar at her desk, the entire surface of which was covered in math quizzes. Most of the students had not done well and she knew she had to reteach and retest. She tried to formulate a plan, but her brain was still buzzing with frustration. Why hadn't they just *listened* to her the first time around? She knew she'd followed every detail of the curriculum; she'd implemented games and tried to make it fun, they'd played *Kahoot* together. Now, her class would be behind the other math teachers in her department who won't be able to get on with the next unit until Cecilia's students could master fractions.

Someone knocked at her door and jiggled the handle. Cecilia instinctively ducked behind her desk. Nothing good ever happened if you let someone in your classroom at lunch, it was like feeding a Gremlin at night, you'd invariably end up losing your free time to unpaid favors or requests. Whoever it was gave up quickly and Cecilia resettled herself.

Cedric had done well on the math quiz, she noted. That was before he had punched the other boy in the face though. *Well, at least I won't have to send a bad grade home with his homework packet*, she thought. She had tried belatedly to intervene on his behalf, but the principal insisted they had a no tolerance policy for fighting and since she'd been injured it was even more imperative they enact a severe punishment.

She stacked the quizzes into a neat pile and wished she had an opportunity to use her 'Dino-mite!' dinosaur stamp she'd bought prior to taking this teaching position. Cecilia recalled her delight when her middle school teachers used quirky stamps or sparkling stickers to reinforce good grades. Her students said the stamp was 'cringe,' so she'd stuffed it into her top drawer along with a hopeful sheet of glitter star stickers.

The bell rang announcing the end of lunch and her momentary peace. She unlocked the door and watched the steady stream of students branch toward her classroom like a single-file tributary, breaking away from the crush of the main hallway's flow.

"Hey, Eddie, you know there's no Bluetooth speakers allowed in the hall! Stefan, get off the skateboard! Sharla, don't trip people! That's not nice. No, I don't want your extra ketchup packets. Wait, no, that doesn't mean you can throw them at people!"

They mostly complied with her commands, but not without casting a glance her way to gauge her reaction.

The freedom of lunchtime always took a while to shake off. Cecilia remembered her own junior high as well-stocked with ice cream sandwiches and Mountain Dew; she subsisted solely on snack foods for most of her adolescence. She knew many of her students ate bags of hot chips that stained their fingers and their homework; she imagined their insides coated with sticky orange and red dust. When they got cranky, depleted of their sugar highs, she offered them her granola bars.

Once the final bell rang, she walked to the center of the room.

"I hope everyone had a great lunch!"

"Did you see? Chux isn't on the list for the *Trash Fighters* tournament."

"Eddie, can you please put your cell phone away?"

"Bro, he's not going."

"Eddie."

The boy slid the phone into his pocket and rolled his eyes at his friend.

"Thank you."

"Alright, before we start with our warm-up, I'd like to collect the homework. Just put it on your desk and I'll pick it up."

Several students bent over to fumble in their backpacks for the surely crumpled piece of looseleaf with their fraction problems copied out. Several others didn't even make the effort to look. Cecilia knew they hadn't done it and felt a wave of disappointment settle into her lower intestine. Combined with reteaching the fraction unit, the number of zeros she'd have to give today made her feel like a failure.

She could hear her mentor teacher: "Your students will rise to the level of rigor you enforce. It's up to you to raise the bar for them — they'll reach it, but it's your job to encourage them."

She collected eight assignments from her twenty students and set them on her desk. Part of her didn't want to share their quiz grades with them; maybe it would be too disheartening. She pretended not to see Eddie checking his phone under his desk and instead pasted on a smile and strode confidently to the front of the room.

"Alright, get your journals out! We are going to do our warm-up."

Cecilia put a mostly unnecessary amount of effort into her warm-ups. They were always visually appealing, timely, and engaging. Today, she played a video of a heron flying over a placid bay — it had gone viral on a nature account she followed and she thought it would bring a sense of calm after the lunchtime storm. She played it on repeat and asked them to quickly write what it made them feel, just one sentence or word. Then, she wanted them to estimate how quickly the heron was traveling and to share their thought process on measuring the speed of a bird, or, for that matter, of any object or creature.

Eddie hadn't raised his head once and Cecilia knew it was time to take up the phone but silently dreaded the confrontation. She walked over to the desk and looked at his blank journal page. He didn't realize she was there until she held out her hand.

"Phone, please."

"Aw, c'mon Miss. I'll do my work."

"Sorry, I already warned you once and we discussed this when everyone signed the social contract for classroom rules."

"I won't do it again."

"Those are the rules you agreed to, Eddie."

He placed his phone in her hand and she put it in the top drawer of her desk.

Another student whispered, "Busted."

Further giggles were suppressed.

Starting class with an altercation, even a minor one, always made the rest of the class period awkward.

She waited until the last ten minutes to hand back the quizzes. A few of the students laughed and nudged each other, a couple looked sufficiently ashamed, and Cecilia caught at least one swear word.

"Alright, as everyone can see, this was a difficult quiz. I don't want you to worry about the grade, because we'll have an opportunity to re-take it. However, it does mean we are spending next week on fractions as well."

A collective groan followed her announcement.

"I know, I know, but it will get you ready for the exam."

More groaning.

"Miss, I'm never gonna need to know fractions. Like, I can do it on my phone."

"I understand you feeling that way, but fractions are an essential tool for understanding advanced math."

"I don't give a shit about math! Fractions are pointless and so is this class."

Cecilia took a deep breath and reminded herself that he was just a kid lashing out because he got a bad grade and felt embarrassed. She mentally planned to repeat her rote speech about the importance of mathematics in the modern world, about all the job opportunities in STEM fields.

What actually came out of her mouth was quite different.

"Well, maybe if you didn't spend all your time fucking around on your phone and actually put some effort into your homework instead of acting like noncompliance is cool, like not giving a shit is awesome, MAYBE THEN we wouldn't have to go over this whole fucking unit again because that isn't going to be fun for EITHER of us. Maybe I don't want to fucking talk about fucking fractions anymore either!"

When she paused for a breath, Cecilia saw twenty sets of eyes staring at her, and suddenly she had the most attention anyone had given her all semester.

The bell rang and no one moved. She didn't know what to do, so Cecilia walked back to her desk and handed Eddie the phone she'd taken up earlier in the period.

"Well, don't be late to your next class."

The students, still in a mild state of shock, gathered their things and opened the door to be absorbed by the hallway. They left Cecilia sitting at her desk with her head in her hands.

She taught her next class in a complete fugue state, then drove home and immediately wrapped herself in a blanket. Supine on her couch, she took a low dose edible and began to scroll mindlessly through her phone. Eventually, her eyes grew fatigued and she passed out on the couch.

When she woke up later, fuzzy and disoriented, it was dark outside and she trudged to her kitchen to heat up leftover pizza in the microwave. The whole studio apartment quickly filled with the dense smell of melted cheese and pepperoni. Cecilia felt disgusted by everything, not least of all herself.

Her phone had several messages and she considered ignoring them, but the first one was from her younger sister and said simply: *Omg, is this u?*

In the text message thread, a fuzzy thumbnail of a YouTube video from an account called: *That's So Cringe* flashed with two or three alternating frames as a preview. Cecilia couldn't make out what it was, but she clicked on it anyway.

A young, attractive guy with his hair dyed bleach blonde and artfully styled to look disheveled began speaking directly to the camera. He had white-toothed charisma that matched his white v-neck shirt, and the viewer was immediately drawn in.

"Alright, so it's Tuesday, which means it's time for fan submissions! And we have a doozy today from a student out in California. The submitter said his teacher 'totally lost it' on them following their bad quiz grades and they caught the whole thing on their phones, because of course they did."

Cecilia's mouth went dry and her armpits began to sweat as she viewed herself shouting the f-word at a group of cowed twelve-year-olds. Watching from a third-person angle felt like a bad dream. She looked like a monster. To make matters worse, there were already thousands of views and a couple hundred comments.

> » All teachers are cunts.
> » This is typical California shit. The liberal dream is alive and well.
> » Fuck the libs.
> » LOLBITCH.
> » I can't believe the state of education today, is this who we employ to teach our children? Is this who we want sharing their morals with the youth of America?
> » My dick is the youth of America.
> » School shooters, do your thing.
> » Definitely a child molester.

Cecilia closed her phone and put it face down. She considered putting it in the freezer and moving to a deserted island where no one would know she yelled at pre-teens. The smell of pizza still permeated every square inch of the space and she opened a window only to be hit in the face with hot, dry winds ripping through the California night. She could find no respite.

The next morning was worse. Her sister sent her several memes now making the rounds. One was of SpongeBob with his hands on his hips, bent over like a squawking chicken, only her audio diatribe was the looped squawking released from her fake SpongeBob self. Her muffled and not very well-recorded voice was reformed into several horrifying golems of internet meme culture.

Cecilia took half an edible before leaving for work, her skin prickling with needles of ice, despite the heat. She had barely entered the school's foyer when the principal stepped into her path.

"I need you to meet with me in my office."

Cecilia just nodded and followed him. He shut the door behind them, Cedric's frightened face in that same room after the fight crossed her mind.

"I think you know what this is about," he said, taking his place of power behind the desk.

Cecilia sat in one of the chairs reserved for naughty students.

"Yes," she whispered.

"We have to nip this in the bud before the parent complaints become overwhelming. So far, we've only had one call, and it may have been a prank, but it seems like someone identified the school. Luckily, we had the identifying comment flagged and removed from YouTube for safety reasons."

"How did you even find out?"

"Google alerts for our school's name."

She nodded.

"There is a protocol for this sort of thing. We'll have to suspend you for the rest of the semester, with pay for now, until everything blows over. We won't mention the video, but you understand that we can't have you teaching children right now. You don't exactly come across as a mentor in that video."

She kept nodding as he explained the next steps then walked alongside her to her classroom to clear out her desk and escorted her out to her car as though she might cause a further scene. They'd hire a sub, no one needed to know anything except that she was taking a leave of absence. She thought about summoning a union rep, she knew she had one, but the thought of explaining the situation to anyone else made her feel sick.

By ten, Cecilia was back in her apartment wrapped in her blanket.

She realized she'd left behind so many things in the classroom, the donated fans, the math manipulatives she'd crowdfunded, the boxes of granola bars that mice would surely find in her absence; there would be no one who knew to run off the mouse that was living under the floorboard. She wondered if any other faculty would even notice that she wasn't there.

Her phone continued to light up with long-term sub notifications, people lining up to take her job, memes from her sister who seemed to be enjoying it all a little too much, and a message from her work friend who asked if they could meet at lunch. Cecilia flipped the phone face down and proceeded to nap intermittently for the rest of the day.

Her sister brought chow mein takeout for dinner that Friday and sat on the floor next to Cecilia's horizontal figure who picked at the noodles with a sideways motion.

"How do you feel?" her sister asked.

"Like a monster. And a failure. Like, I got my degree to help kids learn and here I am losing my temper before my first year ends, my first semester even."

Her sister laughed.

"It's not funny."

"It's a little funny. You really took those little shits to task. What did they do?"

"Nothing. Well, everything. And that smug principal, he already thought I was a bad teacher — too young. He was looking for any excuse to fire me. My department head kept calling me by the wrong name, on purpose, just because he didn't want to learn mine. There wasn't even air-conditioning! I had to buy my own notebooks!"

"There you go, get mad!"

"There are too many expectations! And the kids are mean! And their parents don't care that they're mean, they call and tell *you* to apologize for making their kid curse you out!"

"You need an outlet."

"Like wine?"

"Like something creative, something you can throw your body into. You need to get kinesthetic and out of your own head. Now, will you stop moping, and can we please watch this episode of *The Bachelor*?"

Cecilia started taking a pottery class. Throwing damp clay onto a wheel and using her birdlike arms to mold it into something beautiful felt metaphorical, a rebirth of sorts.

In the end, the memes wrapped up quietly, no one identified her from the video outside of her terminally online sister and the few friends she may have told, the principal kept it mostly to himself and did his part in getting identifying comments removed. Her lack of virality was just lucky, plus most people understood where she was coming from.

She tried not to read the comments on the video. There were close to five hundred now, but when she did check, some of the positive ones about overworked educators had been voted up toward the top, some of the other upvoted comments were from frustrated parents who could understand and empathize. Still, there remained several that called her horrible names, and it made Cecilia feel terrible every time she looked at them, which she sometimes did, like picking at a scab.

When the semester ended a few weeks later, her principal more or less commanded her to return after the holiday break. But Cecilia never went back to teaching math, she never went back into education at all. She found a job working remotely part-time as a transcriptionist for medical documents, and made little clay mugs in her spare time, and, eventually, she forgot that she'd ever said 'fuck' in front of twenty twelve-year-olds. The internet forgot too.

4

Monroe watched the guys swimming in the pool, the aquamarine water glistening with the sheen of endless summer mingling with tanning oil — the sparkling rays dazzled her eyes until she had to look away.

They were filming a video for an athletic clothing brand Monroe hadn't heard of. Surrounding the pool were tripods mounted with the newest iPhones, each one perched precariously close to the water's edge. One guy stood back, adjusting one of the phones to what he considered to be an optimal angle.

They were all tanned, fit, shirtless, and pretending to play HORSE with a floating basketball and plastic hoop affixed to the side of the pool. The water rippled with their exertions. After a few minutes of observation, Monroe realized they didn't know the rules of the game. They were all playacting. The gameplay became muddled and, rather than admit to their lack of knowledge, each of them backed out of the pool onto the steaming concrete where they absorbed themselves instead in viewing the results of their videography attempt played back on their phones.

"Bro, this needs to be angled better."

"You kept splashing near the phone, I couldn't get a better angle."

"You actually have to aim for the basket, what are you even looking at?"

"We gotta do it again, bro."

Resigned, the three of them slid back into the water to flex and mimic having a good time.

Another woman might have been aroused by the scene, but Monroe was inured to their charms. She felt nothing as they showed off their lean muscles in the short swim trunks they were meant to model, all bright colors and flashy designs. Women were drawn to them as one might be drawn to a peacock, mistaking all those showy feathers for something more substantive. But Monroe was not fooled, she knew the gym was the only thing they took seriously — those preciously developed muscles left her cold.

She rolled over onto her stomach, facing away from the pool now. In the adjacent plush lawn, planted with all manner of palm trees and tropical plants that required an almost constant misting in the mid-summer heat, she saw Kassie getting ready to do a #GRWM video for her TikTok audience. She and her part-time assistant set up a tripod and Monroe watched them debate using a ring light. In this oasis, they never had to expose themselves to the harshness of the same sun as everyone else. Here, it was always golden hour.

Kassie started her video in her fairly modest underwear, expensive but gifted, of course, feigning shyness, a coy hand covering her pouting pink lips. Monroe knew as soon as the video went up, one of the first ten comments would be someone demanding her lipstick brand: "Lipstick? Need!" and Kassie would drop an affiliate link in response: "Here you go, babe! Buy it in my shopfront." She'd pin the comment so the next several hundred viewers would know exactly where to go to look exactly like her without having to consider if that shade would complement their own skin tone the same way it complemented Kassie's.

The assistant threw various clothing items from off-camera and Kassie caught each one, then put it on. Each new clothing piece would be a jump cut in the video, eventually resulting in an ideal summer outfit on an idealized body type. Her caption would say something like, "Let's go to brunch!" Except, in reality, Kassie immediately stripped off that outfit and began filming anew, like many a feathered social media phoenix. Sometimes she'd do as many as five in one afternoon.

Now, she huddled with her assistant, their foreheads touching, approving or rejecting each scene. Re-shoots could extend their workdays considerably, so it was best to try and get it on the first go.

Of course, not everyone had an assistant to help, so other people in the house would generally help each other or appear in one another's videos. They created a never-ending time loop of the same people appearing. *Like there's a glitch in the Matrix*, Monroe thought. She'd recently watched the movie for the first time and felt somehow closer to understanding her own life.

Monroe lazily applied another layer of sun bronzing lotion, a product she'd been asked to advertise, and felt it tingle into her skin. "All natural, menthol tingle, no gloves needed," its tube read. Her hands burned red but the tanning lotion coverage wasn't blotchy, she could say that. In her head she composed a review video of herself showing off her back in a strapless dress: the perfect summer glow.

The lingering burn of the lotion brought back a memory of the girl who'd lived in the room next to her before Kassie. The name slipped away, but Monroe remembered everything else. She came from some forgettable town in the Midwest and had all the milk-fed health that came along with it. She was blonde and buxom and had large white teeth that Monroe suspected weren't even caps — the very thought made her sick.

The blonde shilled for a fast fashion brand everyone rose into an uproar about every few months, but simultaneously refused to quit purchasing from.

Monroe had watched her former housemate's videos in the darkness of her own room, breathing very little and running her tongue along the ridges of her mouth. The girl's white teeth and sparkling eyes made her look pure, even when she modeled skintight bandage dresses that would certainly rip after one evening out. The video quality was not particularly good, but she had hundreds of thousands of followers. So did Monroe, but it felt almost like this girl didn't even want them, like she was doing them all a service by spinning around her room in outfit after outfit that you too could order online for less than twenty dollars.

The girl only moved out after a minor controversy featuring one of the items she showed off on her YouTube channel: a large, interlinked metal chain that mimicked an item of the same design made first by an independent artist. Her image subsequently appeared on several influencers' Instagram stories calling for credit to be given to the original creator. All of that still might have blown over with relative ease, had the necklace not been found to also contain mercury. Another YouTuber whose content featured testing glassware for heavy metals while still in the thrift store, tested the necklace as a gag and it went viral. The housemate disappeared back into the open maw of America's breadbasket.

Monroe checked in on her feed about a month after Kassie moved in and she was back at her parents' house selling press-on eyelashes to her high school girlfriends, then Monroe didn't think of her again until now. The tanning lotion could be her mercury necklace, maybe she wouldn't post this one, she decided.

Everyone had a room in the house, that was part of the deal when they signed their contract: free housing, food and gym provided, access to studio space. They decorated it with whatever aesthetic and background they hoped to convey in their diligent social media posting. Most of the guys had Nanoleaf installations that projected garish colors into their living space. Monroe had opted for a 'clean girl aesthetic' — white and beige minimalism, the oatmeal of interior design. She stacked an array of books she'd never read on an acrylic coffee table with fresh white tulips she purchased almost daily from the flower shop. The second they began to brown, she tossed them out. Her compost was that of a funeral parlor, white flowers crushed into dust.

Kassie plopped down on the lounger next to Monroe and sighed heavily.

"Are you not filming today?"

"I did one of those '5-9 before my 9-5' productivity videos of me walking to Pilates and getting coffee after."

"Ugh, so jealous."

"So girlboss."

They both stretched out their long, brown gazelle legs under the yard's softly filtered sun. The guys had ceased playing sports and retreated into the coolness of their rooms where they played *Call of Duty* or *Trash Fighters* until it was time to collect their pre-portioned dinners from the kitchen.

"What's your schedule this week?" Kassie asked.

"I'm doing product reviews for my YouTube channel, several productivity and cleaning videos for TikTok, those are mostly done, Reels re-shares, and editing drafts for next week. I think I have enough content from our trip to Ojai for a part two."

"Tag me in the Ojai Reels."

"For sure."

Monroe looked over at Kassie, reclining languidly with gigantic sunglasses on her face. They had each other's backs, she knew, just like she knew Kassie would never let anyone else see her in those godawful sunglasses for fear of a photo winding up online. She never modeled anything on social media that she truly loved in real life.

"I'm literally so burned out."

Monroe nodded.

"Like, I have no idea how I'm going to squeeze everything into the next week and a half. I have this monstrous pile of clothes in my closet. Last night, I thought it was a person and threw my thrifted Gucci loafer at it. Luckily, I didn't scuff anything, but I am losing my mind. I swear, I almost texted my mom she was right, I should have finished college."

Monroe laughed. None of their parents understood content creation, aesthetics, or social media at large. And the ones who did only used Facebook, maybe Instagram.

"At least your mom still talks to you. Mine told me I was selling my soul along with everything else."

"Jesus!"

"That's who she told me to talk to."

"Do you want to go on a sponsored stay to this resort in Baja with me?"

Monroe lowered her sunglasses to observe her friend better, but Kassie was placidly admiring her new almond-shaped acrylic nails painted with a bright neon paint splatter.

"Another one?"

"It's part of the same parent company as the others."

"Well, hell yeah."

"Let's buy some of those bikinis our asses can munch on."

"Hashtag Pilates ass, perfect."

They both lay back, daydreaming of the richly textured sunset photos for Instagram, the "Come with me to Baja!" captions for TikTok, the quickly cut together restaurant reviews for YouTube. Monroe pulled out her phone and immediately began to message a brand who reached out recently with one of those boilerplate partnership emails. They sold boutique bikinis and vacation wear nice enough to warrant the grid space.

She attached her response, copy and pasted from a Google doc, and a request: Can you get the products to me by next week? I have a great idea for a brand awareness video.

Her phone pinged almost instantly: Of course! We'll ship them this evening via overnight service.

"What are you doing?" Kassie asked. "This is supposed to be our 'no phone' time."

"I'm getting us those bikinis."

Kassie laughed, a deep throaty laugh that always made Monroe think of bygone jazz lounges and French cigarettes. Kassie smoked menthols sometimes, only because of Lana del Rey, and always lit them with one of the matches from the matchbooks she'd collected en masse in Europe, making sure to leave them out on the table like a calling card.

"What do you think of Rob?"

"Which one's Rob?"

"The ex-tech guy."

"I thought he was the ex-college basketball player."

"No, that's Matt."

Monroe shrugged. "He's fine, I guess."

"I might invite him to Baja."

Monroe's face felt hot, though not from the tanning lotion this time.

"I mean, it's a suite, there are four bedrooms. We can use the extra one for filming."

"Yeah, if you want to," Monroe tried to sound casual.

"The goal, of course, is to only use two of the bedrooms," Kassie teased.

Monroe forced a laugh that sounded like a groan.

Baja was hot, hotter than Los Angeles, but Monroe straightened her spine and refused to wilt. She'd already filmed a video that morning outlining her skincare routine and SPF 50 was part of it. Kassie and Rob walked ahead of her, Kassie wore an all-white sundress and Rob wore salmon-colored shorts and white rubber Crocs on his feet; Monroe thought his pale arms were sure to burn in the sun. Rob also kept saying "Sheeesh" in a high-pitched voiced that Monroe found increasingly grating.

The resort Kassie partnered with was all white stucco which lent a lightness to the walls and natural coolness in the rooms. In the lobby, large palms made everything feel lush and private. The sound of running water trickled from somewhere Monroe couldn't place. Kassie walked confidently to the white marble countertop and checked them in. There was a flurry of activity behind the register and welcome drinks were produced for all three of them, compliments of the house.

Monroe's drink was orange and fizzy and tasted of the creamsicles she remembered from her youth. They carried the cocktail glasses along with them for a tour of the grounds while the bellboys loaded their luggage onto a metal cart and disappeared into some behind the scenes elevator. When Monroe looked back, there was no trace that they'd ever stood in the lobby at all.

The concierge finally walked them to their palatial suite. It had the four bedrooms with ensuite bathrooms Kassie had promised, a living area and kitchenette, and a large balcony that overlooked the ocean. The balcony had a private plunge pool and hot tub. Monroe hid the fact that she was duly impressed by taking another sip of her drink; the sweetness coated her tongue and made it feel hairy.

Rob ostentatiously tipped the concierge and the bellboys, making sure to say: "And a little something for you," when they arrived with the luggage moments later. Monroe turned to roll her eyes at Kassie, but her friend seemed impressed with his ridiculous showing of twenties.

Kassie took the largest bedroom, the other three were similarly sized, but before Monroe could take the one next to Kassie, Rob threw his bag on the bed.

"Let's get ready to go down to the pool," Kassie commanded.

"I can't wait to see the setup, it looks sick. I wonder if they do chlorine or saltwater."

"Saltwater surely."

As they continued to carry forth on the merits of pool water, Monroe remained quiet. In the privacy of her own room, the furthest one from Kassie, Monroe turned on the air conditioning and flopped onto the bed which also had all white linens, of course. She slid her gold sandals off and opened Instagram, navigating over to Kassie's profile. Monroe's white manicure blurred together with the background of the room and the images on the screen as she slid it rapidly downwards, seeking the seemingly endless bottom of her friend's profile.

Her hand grew tired of swiping before she'd scrolled down far enough to reach Kassie's unsaturated, unposed six-year-old images. Here, Monroe knew, you were more likely to find the real person behind the social media account, if they left themselves exposed. Monroe had begun to systematically wipe her own pages years ago — a viewer could only scroll back through two carefully curated years on her Instagram.

In one photo, a young Kassie was laughing at a party. The other people's faces were dark and blurred, but Kassie was a radiant light amidst their group. She had on too much makeup and a sequined dress that made Monroe cringe a little, it looked like something from a suburban mall. In another photo, Kassie posed under changing fall foliage, wearing a beige sweater, oversized plaid scarf, jeans, and suede boots that went over her calves. Her pose was awkward; she reached one arm toward the tree, the other she held with her hand popped out like a child performing 'I'm a Little Teapot.' Monroe was surprised by how much older she looked, despite her childlike affectations. She used two fingers to zoom in closer on Kassie's face, pre-Botox and lip fillers, and felt something like love.

Outside her bedroom, she could hear her friend's throaty laugh and Rob saying 'Sheeeesh' for the fiftieth time that day. She put her phone face down on the bed and threaded her body into one of the barely-there swimsuits she'd received in due haste, followed by a sheer cover-up, then slid the gold sandals back onto her feet.

"Ready!" she called, swinging the door open.

Their first half an hour at the pool was taken up with snapping photos. Kassie and Monroe posed in their swimsuits, drinking another creamsicle cocktail, laughing behind their sunglasses. Even Monroe had to admit Rob was willing to work to get the angles, he bent and crouched and laid fully on the ground; he directed them to get in the infinity pool and clink their drinks together with a backdrop of the ocean. "Yes, that's great," he encouraged. Other guests of the hotel paused in the well-trod path from pool to bar to stand and watch the sleek young women hold themselves aloft in the most flattering poses they could manage. They took over a hundred photos, some with Kassie and Monroe together, some separately, and Rob wasn't in any of them.

At least he knows his role, Monroe thought.

Kassie snapped a few photos of him in the pool afterward and bought him a thank-you margarita. Once they'd gotten the photos and the sun reached the impossible zenith that always cast unflattering shadows, they all sighed with collective relief — they could finally enjoy themselves. They stretched out on the sun loungers, side by side, sipping drinks and silently editing the photos on their phones. Monroe tried not to be annoyed that Rob put himself in the middle again, only because he'd taken some very good swimsuit photos for her did she let her frustration simmer in a silent part of her, for now.

She'd left Kassie's Instagram open and surreptitiously zoomed in on another picture of her, this time holding a collie in the snow. Monroe propped herself up on her elbow to examine the woman in the sun lounger with her lithe body, contoured face, and recently lightened hair. The girl holding the collie was wearing a plaid headband.

Rob sat up suddenly, blocking her view, and leaned over toward Kassie in a way Monroe would have described as leering.

"What do y'all want to get into tonight? I heard there are some sick clubs down by the water."

"There's one in the resort."

"Oh yeah? Should we hit it up? I bet we can get bottle service."

"Of course we can."

Monroe turned her attention to a couple swimming together in the water. They were both wearing swim styles she considered to be last season, or perhaps even before that, but they were splashing lightly together in the deep end, laughing. They both had wet hair and appeared unconcerned about preserving it for photos. One of them kept leaning back to laugh and Monroe could see all the tendons in her neck. Like the swimsuit, her breasts were larger than what was considered fashionable at the moment, but the way they swayed in the water like buoys the color of cool milk made Monroe reconsider the trend. The couple climbed out of the pool and walked toward the bar. They didn't squeeze out their swimsuits or self-consciously readjust and Monroe watched the water drip and pool underneath their feet.

"What do you think, Monroe?"

She realized Kassie had asked her a question.

"About what?"

"Which restaurant we should check out, the one with the views or the one with the seafood tower?"

Monroe considered the potential for content before announcing, "Seafood tower."

"That's what I was thinking too!"

Rob pouted in between them, he'd clearly been hoping for views. Monroe laid back on her sun lounger, content with seeing the frown line appear between his eyes. At some point, Kassie extracted several glossy magazines from her bag and passed one to Monroe, no one spoke for the rest of the afternoon.

The seafood tower that came to their table that evening was displayed on two levels — the bottom platter was almost entirely composed of raw oysters, the top was crab legs and prawns and ceviche tucked into abalone shells. Upon its arrival, Monroe and Kassie immediately stood up and began filming it. Kassie climbed up on her chair to get a bird's eye view, wobbling in her stiletto heels. Once they'd had their fill, it was time to eat.

"I'm not eating the oysters," Rob protested.

"Haven't you had one before?"

"Yeah, but not like, in Mexico."

"They're the same thing."

"Are they?"

Monroe rolled her eyes as Kassie continued to try and convince him. He eventually relented, of course he did, but only after extracting a promise that Kassie would keep an eye on him that night in case of potential food poisoning. He literally winked and nudged her, and, to Monroe's horror, Kassie laughed her throaty laugh.

The oysters Monroe ate that evening had no flavor at all.

She went to bed early, despite the others' insistence that she stay up and try the bottle of Mezcal the hotel had gifted them. Instead, she lay in the silent darkness of her well-insulated bedroom looking at the pictures Kassie had posted that day. She zoomed in on her friend's face, the coy smile she always wore online. Then, she scrolled all the way back to the end of her feed again to find the genuine smile, the one with all the teeth and tinted lip gloss from the drugstore. She fell asleep with the phone on her chest.

Monroe woke early and filmed the sunrise, then filmed herself doing a quick yoga session on the balcony, then making a Nespresso in the large kitchenette and enjoying it in her gauzy robe with a view of the ocean. Just as she was splicing the videos together and adding a trending song, Kassie and Rob both walked out of Kassie's room. Monroe bobbled her phone and let out a small cry of panic. Kassie caught sight of her on the balcony and realized they'd been caught; she smiled sheepishly and came outside to join her. Monroe felt what was left of her morning calm disperse.

"Hey."

"Good morning."

"Were you up filming stuff?"

"Just the regular morning routine, you know the drill. I'm going to post it around noon if that's okay with your schedule. I feel like people know we are here together though."

"Yeah, I am just trying to keep Rob out of it. I don't need the hate messages again. Any time I post a man on my feed it's all 'whore' this and 'slut' that. He understands though."

"I bet he does."

Kassie smirked. "We didn't *do* anything. Well, we did *some* things, but not anything. Really."

Monroe shrugged. "He's fine, I mean, he's boring but harmless."

"Oh, he's okay. He talked to me last night about his goals with leveraging his online platform to create a startup."

"A startup for what?"

"Disruption of the status quo, or something like that."

"That's what they all say. They all want to disrupt something."

"Did you use the Nespresso machine?"

Monroe raised her cooling mug to indicate she had.

"I definitely need a coffee, I barely slept."

"An espresso martini to wipe it all out."

Kassie laughed with a lightness that indicated she'd ceased listening and went inside where Rob handed her one of the rough earthenware mugs, identical to the one in Monroe's hands. Kassie leaned her body against the countertop at a classic forty-five-degree angle pose, using her small, high breasts as well as her sculpted legs to her advantage. They were speaking now, but Monroe couldn't hear them.

She looked down at her phone — she'd stashed her morning video in the drafts folder, along with the seafood tower video from last night. They'd brought out a chocolate mousse with sparklers at the end of dinner and she knew it would be a video capable of inspiring envy.

All the other tabs open on her phone were private windows of Kassie's social media pages: Twitter, Instagram, TikTok. Monroe was browsing them with her alt accounts, swiping her way back in time on their balcony with a view of the undulating ocean. Below her, people had begun to crowd the pool loungers with towels, walked along the beach hand in hand, and Monroe read five-year-old tweets.

There was one tweet, well, several really, but one in particular, where Kassie expressed an unpopular political view. She also endorsed a male influencer who was caught up in a sexual harassment scandal and had, by now, been found fully guilty of everything. Kassie called him a 'friend,' who would 'never do something like that.' She didn't understand why Kassie hadn't employed an app to delete her Twitter history; Monroe had been using one for years, though she supposed no one really expected to be taken down by Twitter anymore. Who was even still on that site?

Monroe looked back through the sliding glass door to watch Kassie rubbing Rob's pale arm. She took screenshots of the tweets, then closed every tab, and sipped her now lukewarm coffee.

She already knew what they were going to say when they poked their heads out. She sensed them behind her, holding hands.

"Hey M," Rob called out.

She turned slowly to face them both.

"We're going to go down to some of the shops today. I figured you wouldn't want to come," Kassie said.

Monroe wanted to ask, 'why would you think that?' But she didn't. She understood her place had shifted during the night, like an earthquake you only felt in your dreams.

"Yeah, not really my thing. I'll be at the pool. Y'all come find me later."

Monroe slipped out while they were getting ready. She wore a cerulean one piece that was cut open all the way down to her belly button paired with her gold sandals. She covered her expression with oversized secondhand Prada sunglasses. In the elevator's cold reflective surface she observed herself until the doors opened, breaking her body in two.

The lobby had filled up with couples checking in at the large marble reception desk. The sight of so many happy people made Monroe want to close her eyes. Instead, she strode purposefully to the small store that sold towels monogrammed with the hotel's logo, beach reads, bottles of overpriced water, and other sundry items one might prefer to purchase rather than make the long return to one's room for.

Monroe selected a book, something romantic with an oversaturated cover illustration of a woman in a bikini. She walked out to the pool gripping it under her arm, intending to read the entire thing in one day. When was the last time she'd read a book at all? She wouldn't even look at her phone, she'd be utterly absorbed when the two lovebirds returned.

In a repetition of the prior afternoon, she splayed herself out on a lounger. A woman in a bikini top and sarong approached and asked if she'd like anything from the bar.

"An espresso martini, please."

The day passed in a pleasant haze and Monroe did finish the entire book. She felt an immense feeling of accomplishment and resisted the urge to share it online for a cheap dopamine hit. She was a little tipsy from drinking on an empty stomach all afternoon, but not unpleasantly so. She thought she might totter back to the room to clean up for dinner.

On her way back to the lobby, she passed the window of one of the resort's many restaurants. Several couples were having a late lunch since time meant very little here, and Monroe felt an unfamiliar pang of envy. Then, silhouetted between two potted palms, she saw Rob lean over to kiss Kassie's hand. Between them was a shared platter of oysters and a bottle of sparkling wine chilling in a metal bucket beside the table. Monroe's stomach lurched; she hurried past them, immediately taking the elevator back up to their room.

Fully alone, she logged into her alt account and navigated to a well-known gossip and meme account. She sent the screenshots of Kassie's tweets, then leaned back against the wall gasping.

Once she'd recovered, Monroe showered slowly, using all the hotel's provided soaps and lotions. She exfoliated her legs with a raw sea sponge and dried her hair with a microfiber towel. At least she'd gotten a decent tan today, it could be her souvenir.

She packed her bags, carefully placing everything back in their assigned pastel packing cubes, her wet swimsuit in a plastic bag, and tossed the romance novel onto Kassie's bed on her way down to the lobby where she asked for a cab to the airport.

Neither Kassie nor Rob came back to the Los Angeles house from Baja and Monroe didn't hear from either of them again. Kassie's name was trending on Twitter for close to a week before she closed her account down for good, Instagram and TikTok followed shortly after. Still, Monroe knew Kassie would reinvent herself, she'd be fine — she wasn't like Monroe who lacked the skills necessary for survival.

Two weeks later, a new girl from Sweden moved into Kassie's old room. Monroe observed her delicately unpacking three or four boxes — she had so few personal possessions. She set a small stack of books on the nightstand and laid out her ten or so pairs of shoes along the foot of the bed. The sparseness made Monroe feel something like pity and she walked down the hallway to introduce herself.

TikTok House: From Dream to Dust

The doors closed on the famed Los Angeles influencer house that made household names of TikTokkers like KassieTellsU, Monroevia, BBoyz, and skyrocketed the group's YouTube channel: *That's So Cringe* to one of the most viewed on the platform. Unfortunately, the investors who had helped to fund the house's less aesthetic qualities, like rent and food (we hear they even had daily meal delivery), were shut down for running a crypto mining service out of their second Los Angeles home. It came to the attention of the city due to an overexertion of their particular house on the Los Angeles suburb's power grid. [...]

Click to read more >

**Trash Fighters Unofficial
@tfunofficial:** *(Un)official
rankings come out today!*
3,050 people like this.

**Toad @princetoadstool replying to
@tfunofficial:** *aw man, don't make
me change my bio line!*
Bio: Top 10 Trash Fighters Player.

**Porky Dig @PorkyDig replying to
@tfunofficial:** *Let's see it boys!*
5,231 people like this.

**Trash Fighters Unofficial
@tfunoffial:**
1. MumsTheWord
2. DumpsterDivrrr
3. numbChux
4. Flip
5. RaeofLight
6. TheNoodler
7. TrashKing
8. PorkyDig
9. MinorCharacter
10. LeashLaws
20,462 people like this.

**Toad @princetoadstool replying to
@tfunoffial:** *I'll always be top
10 in my heart…*
Bio: Top 25 Trash Fighters Player.

The year's most exclusive and, arguably, most important *Trash Fighters* tournament took place in a huge auditorium housed in one of the many casinos along the Las Vegas Strip. It was part of a three-day video gaming extravaganza, a long weekend that brought thousands of visitors to the city to compete and spectate. *Trash Fighters* wasn't the only game featured, dozens of other fighting games had full weekend-long brackets and events; however, *Trash Fighters* had the added cache of being billed as the newest addition to this long running competitive e-sports event. The game was somewhat begrudgingly admitted to the lineup only after *Trash Fighters* was a confirmed indie hit in the online streaming community.

There were a few already well-known streamers: MumsTheWord and DumpsterDivrrr, who got the game on the map, but a swath of new faces soon graced everyone's streams. On Friday nights, Mums started organizing online tournaments that drew a huge following. Suddenly, *Trash Fighters* was trending on social media even though the game had come out years before.

numbChux and PorkyDig were some of the known streamers who began playing during that time. Chux even did a twenty-four-hour stream where he did nothing aside from tirelessly practice his main *Trash Fighters* character — a raccoon who threw banana peels and had a turbo move called 'rabies' — against any of his Twitch subscribers who wanted to play against him. When he finally entered one of Mums' tournaments, he won handily. Chux became a vocal advocate for *Trash Fighters* on social media and this Vegas tournament should have been the culmination of all his work, but Chux wasn't there.

In a hotel room, PorkyDig, whose real name was Brian, had connected his gaming console to the hotel's large television. Endlessly replayed visions of beautiful people eating in the hotel's many restaurants and laughing in the pool were subsumed by the *Trash Fighters* loading screen. Though he had an expansive view of the bright lights of Las Vegas, he pulled the blackout curtains shut in order to avoid any screen glare.

His roommate, LFGordon, was also a streamer who often live commentated *Trash Fighters* matches — he was one of the scene's most notorious hype men and Porky's best streaming buddy. They both loved wrestling, a holdover from their youth, and tailored their online personas in the same way. They often streamed *Trash Fighters* together. It had started with *Trash Fighter Friday*, then they added *Trashy Tuesdays*, but Porky had enough subscribers now that he quit his restaurant job and streamed almost every day. Recently, Porky also gained an energy drink brand's sponsorship who now handled most of his travel and event registration payments.

"Hey man, thanks for lugging the setup on the plane," Gordon called from the bathroom where he was carefully applying gel eye masks so as to not look puffy on screen tomorrow.

"I have a separate suitcase for it now, so it wasn't as bad as when we went to Austin. They got us a better room this time too."

Gordon joined him and they sat on the edge of the white hotel bed together. They navigated to the game's startup menu, and both smiled as the ensemble of playable characters appeared before them. Gordon always played the crow character whose main move was to peck your eyes; he also regurgitated toxic pools designed to sink his opponents and had a wing attack that dealt maximum damage by creating a wind tunnel but could only be used if you had enough space. Sometimes he played the opossum character whose main move, 'hysterical hiss,' had impressive knockback. Gordon thought the opossum played a little slower overall though, and he liked the swooping freedom of his crow avatar. Porky, like Chux, played the raccoon character and wasted no time in making his choice.

The friends played together for a while, warming up their hands and hurling light insults.

"So, you think Chux is gonna show up?"

"I dunno."

"He definitely got invited."

"Yeah, so did I."

"Speaking of that, how does it feel to be Top 10?"

"They only ever invite the Top 10, and it doesn't even mean anything. They just want to make sure we show up for content. We still have to play all the way through the bracket with the peasants."

"I know, but..."

"Look, I don't really give a shit if Chux shows up or out or not at all. I mean, his little disappearing act just gives me more of an opportunity to win. I can roll over anyone else here. So, if you help me practice against the crow, I have a shot at number one if he's actually pussed out."

Gordon didn't argue, but he secretly hoped Chux would show up. It would be hard to hype the crowd without him. Gordon also knew his friend liked to be a heel online, he trolled people and tried to make them angry — the Porky vs Chux fans were particularly divided. Chux was the *Trash Fighters* golden boy, while Porky smoked weed on stream and had gotten suspended from Twitch a few times for his behavior. Porky was someone people either loved or hated, versus Chux who was thought of as wholesome and generous. Gordon wasn't looking forward to commentating a match between Porky and Chux — his own loyalty felt divided.

"Have you thought about like, toning it down for this tournament?"

"Toning what down?"

"The whole wrestler 'heel' thing, the menacing stares and sarcastic remarks."

"That's my brand."

"Being a douchebag?"

"People love a villain. I'm like Gaston."

"Gaston?"

"Big, brawny, bitchy, you know. I don't need people to root for me, but they can't stay mad if I outplay everyone. Which is why I need to practice," he shot an accusing look at Gordon.

"No one deflects like Gaston, gets to project like Gaston," Gordon hummed.

PorkyDig was, in fact, a large guy and, in person, he was quite intimidating. But people had a hard time recognizing him outside of his low-ceilinged bedroom where he sat in the dim purple light with his gaming trophies in the background taunting fellow players in a booming voice.

He referred to his Twitch followers as 'The Pig Pen,' and they took the moniker seriously. They'd type: *Get oinked*! whenever he did something impressive and repeated sayings in Twitch chat: *Spam this snout to help Porky out! Spam this pig for PorkyDig!* with the corresponding pig emojis. When Porky went to any competition, his fans showed up in droves wearing the tell-tale rubber snouts over their noses.

Gordon and Porky played well into the night. Gordon cycled through both the crow and opossum against Porky's raccoon, stopping only to order chicken tenders and fries from the room service menu.

"Chicken tendies!" Porky cried in a high falsetto when they heard room service's knock at the door.

The smell of fried food filled the room immediately and they set their controllers aside, their fingers numb from staying curled around the buttons.

"This is actually pretty good," Gordon acknowledged.

"Yeah, I said they got us a nice hotel room this time."

"Who do you have to play first tomorrow?"

"Some no names. I'm the strongest player in my first round of pools, I'm not worried. Then it's on to the real shit."

"I have to commentate a mid-morning block."

"It might be mine."

Gordon wondered briefly if he could switch. Porky always watched the recordings back and sometimes asked why Gordon couldn't hype him more.

Gordon noticed Porky posting a picture of their 'chicken tendies' on his Twitter.

Chicken tendies power up, he wrote underneath.

The post would have over a thousand likes in the morning.

They decided to call it a night and Gordon retired to the bathroom to do his several step skin-care routine while Porky collapsed face down on the bed.

They entered the venue together the following morning. Porky wore his energy drink sponsor's jersey — they'd put his name on the back — and loose sweatpants with slide-on black rubber sandals. Gordon wore skinny jeans and a blazer over a patterned button down, he'd debated a bow tie but decided to save it for the grand finals instead.

At the entrance to the convention center was a massive registration area where people collected their lanyards and badges. Gordon was always a little surprised to see how many people bought spectator badges for events like this. The *League of Legends* international tournament in San Francisco always sold out quickly and garnered a crowd so huge that people who didn't manage to get spectator passes could watch their favorite teams outside the venue on huge flatscreen TVs set up explicitly for this purpose. Although *Trash Fighters* was much more indie, they walked the same hallowed halls as *Street Fighter* and *Mortal Kombat*.

Almost immediately someone stopped and approached them.

"Hey man, can I get a selfie?"

Porky smirked, "Sure."

The guy who had approached put on a rubber pig snout and angled his camera to make his height look comparable to Porky's immense stature. They snapped a couple of photos.

"Good luck today, Pork!"

The fan's friends approached him to admire the selfie and Gordon wondered if he'd wear the snout all day now.

Porky and Gordon picked up their respective badges and walked under a welcome banner into a massive auditorium, one of several being utilized that day, where long tables were set up with gaming consoles and screens, one after the other. At the back of the auditorium, two stages were set up with consoles and modern gaming chairs facing one another like a modern-day showdown. The players would be on stage, their battles broadcast on a large screen for everyone to see. Rows of chairs backed up to the long tables that preceded the stage where players were playing their pools sets already.

Gordon rushed over to the production area to see where he was needed; Porky immediately found an open practice console and sat down. People flocked around him and someone asked if he wanted to play. He nodded and proceeded to cycle through volunteers until he was called for his first match.

Porky had to mask his annoyance when the production team informed him he wouldn't be featured on the main stage, which meant his match wouldn't be streamed to the thousands of online viewers. He reminded himself it would allow him to practice without simultaneously performing for the camera; he could focus, it was a good thing. The muscles in his face relaxed a little.

He heard Gordon's voice over the microphone cracking some joke that made the other commentator laugh. His friend's popularity sometimes grated on Porky's nerves. He walked over to the gaming setup he'd been assigned — a teenager with greasy hair was already sitting there, still rubbing the sleep from his eyes.

"First time in Vegas?" Porky joked.

The contender fixed a scowl on his face and Porky watched it disappear once he realized who he was playing against.

They played through a 'best of three' set, and Porky easily took the first two games. He fist-bumped the teenager who looked more exhausted than anything else.

Bring on the next one, Porky thought to himself, *I'll run them all over.*

He ended up placing first in his pool and stayed on the winner's side of the bracket, his high placement ensuring he wouldn't need to play again until the following day. He was officially off-duty. The teenager he'd beat in the first round got eliminated, but he still asked for Porky's photo on the way out of the venue.

Porky headed to the VIP players' area set up in one of the hotel's smaller conference rooms. The invited players were given access and he showed his lanyard to the person at the door who ushered him in. Inside, the room was practically dark, all the lights were off, no one could have discerned the time of day. The oxygenated air common to all Vegas casinos blew through the vents. Consoles were set up on low tables along modern, red velvet sofas. There were full arcade cabinet buildouts where people played old school *Street Fighter* and *Star Wars* pinball. A bar was set up at the back and Porky ordered a beer.

He recognized a few of the other players. They were allowed to bring in their partners, so 'normie' people were mingling respectfully as though it were a children's birthday party during nap time — no one wanted to distract the players still competing. Tomorrow, this would also be the space to drown your sorrows, but today, no one seemed to have suffered any catastrophic upsets as of yet.

"Porky!" someone called.

He turned and recognized DumpsterDiverrr, another top ranked *Trash Fighters* player.

"Dumpster!"

"You make it out of pools?"

"First place."

"Cheers to that!"

Porky clinked his glass, downed the rest of his beer, and asked for another one.

"I always forget you can tank better than the rest of us," his friend indicated the empty glass.

"It's true, I'm a barbarian."

"So, you worried about anyone tomorrow?"

"Is the schedule even out yet?"

"Not officially. Have you seen Chux?"

Porky felt a small surge of panic, "No. Is he here?"

"I don't know. He was scheduled to be in pools, but I haven't checked to verify it. I know people really want him to play, but I also get needing time for yourself."

"I guess he isn't taking it as seriously as he used to."

True to his name, Porky couldn't resist a dig at his absent competitor.

"He won the last tournament."

"Hey, I'd be scared I couldn't do it again too."

DumpsterDiverrr gave him a questioning look but didn't press the conversation any further.

Porky had a third beer and then a fourth. Eventually, pools play ended, and the room filled up with other victors. He followed some of his fellow VIPs into the gambling area of the casino. No one knew what time it was, and they started playing slot machines as something of a joke, but the bright lights and quick wins drew them in. The slot machine cabinets, themed with *Marvel* characters and fairytales, recalled a hazy childhood they still longed to recapture. They sat there for what seemed like hours in the smoky haze, letting women in short black skirts bring them drinks on trays. Porky lost one hundred dollars on slots, but Dumpster lost almost five hundred playing just three rounds of blackjack.

Porky's phone pinged with a Discord message and he noticed it was almost one in the morning — he had to play at eleven.

He tried to tell Dumpster he needed to get some sleep, but they were in Vegas and no one wanted to go to bed. The casino's lighting never changed, regardless of the hour, and their internal clocks were skewed. Someone said there was a club on the next floor that played music until three. Porky let himself be dragged along. A few fans coming back from their nights out recognized them moving in a pack across the casino floor, but Dumpster put on his sunglasses and pretended to be security.

"No photos, no photos please!"

He ushered Porky ahead of him, everyone in their group laughing.

The fans who had wanted a selfie were left to scowl at their empty camera rolls until they went off to drink Red Bull and vodkas and complain on Twitter.

The club itself was small, but the dance floor was half on the ground, half an elevated catwalk along a fake Viking ship. People were already crawling all over it like drunk pirates, on the floor people gyrated their bodies to a mediocre DJ.

"Valhalla!" Dumpster cried out.

They went to the bar and took Jaeger shots. Though he felt self-conscious being a head taller than almost everyone, his friends immediately began throwing their alcohol-loosened limbs around and Porky tried to join in.

A woman approached them and started talking to Dumpster. Porky couldn't hear what they were saying over the music, but his friend laughed and pointed in Porky's direction. The woman walked over. She wore a fitted silver dress that reflected the light and made her look like a disco ball. It was paired with knee-high patent leather boots, her hair was cut into a bob and dyed neon purple.

"Hey, he said you're PorkyDig."

"Yeah, I am."

"Cool, I watch your stream all the time."

Porky just nodded; he could feel the sweat streaming down the sides of his temples.

"You want to dance?"

Again, he nodded silently in response.

There wasn't much space to move, so they backed away from the bar a little to gyrate together. Dumpster shot Porky a thumbs up from the sideline.

"What's your name?" Porky shouted.

"Molly."

He couldn't think of anything else to say afterwards, so he just tried to focus on not stepping on her feet. He wanted to tell her she reminded him of this hot tub streamer on Twitch that always wore wigs, but she probably didn't know who Anthem was, and, besides, he didn't really want to talk for fear that Molly might stop dancing with him. It felt rude somehow to feel her small, hard body pressing against his without words.

"Do you want a drink?" he finally asked.

"Vodka soda."

Porky walked over to the bar and ordered two vodka sodas. He brought them back to Molly, who, he noticed, was also sweating now.

"It's hydrating," she shouted.

"I'm not sure that's how it works."

She laughed.

"You're probably right. But I keep telling myself if I drink liquor cut with water I'll somehow be able to pretend to be functional tomorrow."

"Are you going to the tournament?"

"Yeah."

"Cool."

Porky assumed she was a commentator, like Gordon, or she played one of the imported puzzle games.

"Yeah, it's weird isn't it? Kind of like the internet come to life, seeing people you recognize from watching Twitch or YouTube just hanging out at the bar. It's surreal."

"People keep asking me for selfies," Porky couldn't resist bragging a little.

Molly sipped her drink. "Does it annoy you?"

"Not really. Only when they ask after I lose a match. I feel like I can't ask for space though because they're the reason I'm here, part of why I have enough money to travel for stacked tournaments to play in-person. I feel like I owe them."

"Yeah, I know what you mean. Guys in my channel always DM me to ask if I'm single and if I don't respond or if I say it's not their business, they usually call me a name and unsubscribe."

"That's awful." He paused, "But also, *are* you single?"

"I wouldn't be dancing with you if I wasn't."

They took their drinks further into the dance floor and moved together amongst the other sweating bodies. Porky couldn't spot Dumpster and wondered if his friends had left him, until he heard someone cry out, "Valhalla!"

and turned to see Dumpster hanging off the side of the Viking ship. Someone else was taking videos, then they disappeared again into the crush, jumping up and down along with the DJ's beat drops.

He and Molly danced until the DJ took a break; they were both sweaty and smiling.

"I should probably turn in, I've got an early morning," Molly said.

"Same, yeah. I do too."

"Well, I'll see you at the venue tomorrow."

"Sure."

She shook out her hair and walked off the dance floor, back into the casino, taking all the light with her.

Porky didn't think to get her number or Instagram handle until she was already gone.

He woke the next morning to Gordon prodding him hard in the back, his fingers sinking into Porky's meaty flesh that smelled of old booze and casino cigarettes.

"Dude, DUDE! You need to get up or you're gonna miss bracket play."

Porky rolled over, a trail of saliva running from his mouth back to the pillow. Gordon, who had already been up for an hour primping, recoiled.

"You look grotesque."

"Thanks," Porky mumbled.

"You better hope they don't stream any of your matches."

Porky wiped his face and stumbled to the bathroom where he vacillated between needing to vomit or not. He chugged cup after cup of water from the tiny plastic mouthwash glasses provided by the hotel, then gave up and stuck his head fully underneath the spigot.

"They have Voss in the mini fridge," Gordon offered.

"How long do I have until I'm due downstairs."

"Maybe ten minutes? You have to check in."

Porky changed into a different pair of sweatpants, washed his face, and ran his damp fingers through his short hair.

"Here," Gordon offered him some cologne. "You don't want to live up to the 'smelly gamer' stereotype."

He applied a little, knowing it wouldn't mask his four AM bedtime, then rushed out to the elevators.

"Good luck!"

Gordon drank a complimentary bottle of Voss and decided today he *would* wear the bow tie.

Porky's rubber slides made a classic flopping sound as he rushed to the check-in desk.

"PorkyDig."

"Man, your set is in like two minutes!"

"Yeah, I know, just check me in."

The tournament volunteer did so, and Porky rushed past several people who tried to speak with him, dodged players on the floor like a *Frogger* level, and eventually made it to the stage. Of course, he was on the main stage, which meant it would be streamed. He groaned out loud.

One of the tournament volunteers was speaking into a headset, "Yeah, he's here. We're starting."

Porky plugged his controller into the console and felt a wave of calm center him as *Trash Fighters* booted up on stream and he moved the cursor over his preferred raccoon character. He felt all the comfort of returning to an old friend.

He saw his competitor's tag was: DramaLlama.

Without looking up, he called across the screen setup: "Hey man, sorry I'm late. Give me a minute to warm up my hands and we can go."

"Sure thing."

The wave of calm crashed when he realized he recognized the voice. He peered over the large monitors separating them and came face to face with Molly. He was certain he was hallucinating from the high concentration of casino oxygen.

"Molly?"

She looked up, brushing her purple hair back from her face, and smiled. His first rather unfair thought was, why didn't she look as green as he did?

"Hey."

"Are you... you're playing me?"

"Yeah."

"Did you know that last night?"

"I knew we were potentially playing today, but not first up."

His second, and somewhat angrier, thought was that he'd been sabotaged. His hands shook as they struck stages and finally chose which backdrop to fight on. He wasn't even surprised when her bird came swooping down to challenge him — the one character he still struggled against, of course.

The first game, Molly won handily. She got a turbo wing blast off quickly and sent Porky's raccoon flying, he couldn't regain the upper hand. In the second game, Porky steadied himself and kept his character a close distance from Molly's, making sure she didn't have a chance to use any of her boosted long-range attacks. His raccoon bites and short-range projectiles eventually knocked Molly's crow off the stage and he won. Now tied, one to one, they each had an opportunity to take a win. Porky knew he'd be mercilessly mocked in Twitch chat for 'losing to a girl,' in fact, he suspected it was already happening. They'd call him 'washed' and lump him in with the absent numbChux, who had yet to show his face in Vegas.

Porky closed his eyes and tried to concentrate on the W.

As soon as their characters dropped into the stage, Molly's bird attacked Porky's raccoon with her eyeball peck. Porky was thrown, no one used that attack in competitive gameplay, and he proceeded to play the entire game from behind. They were dead even until both characters were knocked offstage, and Porky's raccoon lacked the wings to fly back. He watched his character plummet down into an unknown depth with a pathetic squeal while Molly's crow landed daintily on the edge of the stage.

He stood solemnly, fist bumped Molly, who looked radiant with the flush of a first big win, and then walked directly to the bathroom where he threw up.

Gordon came downstairs to pandemonium. The entire commentator booth was discussing PorkyDig getting upset by some new player. They were laughing and Gordon felt a sympathy he quickly masked with professionalism. It was almost his turn to commentate, but he checked Twitter and searched 'PorkyDig + Vegas' to find a slew of comments mocking his friend's loss interspersed with a few fans complaining that he wasn't friendly toward them in Vegas, and they were his *real* fans! How could he treat them like that?

Gordon closed the app and sighed.

"Hey, nice bowtie Gordo!" his co-commentator, LilCheez, offered.

"Thanks, man."

"Did you see your boy get wrecked by that anime chick?"

"I didn't, but I heard it was one for the ages."

"I saw Dumpster's photos from last night, I think they had a rough one. Probably not the best idea if you're aiming to actually win."

"Always drink *after* you've been eliminated."

"Exactly."

A tournament organizer spoke into their headpieces, "Three, two, one. You're live!"

"Aaaaand we're back! I'm LFGordon with LilCheez here to get y'all hyped for Vegas, baby! Put an LFG in chat if you're ready for some sick *Trash Fighters* play!"

From the bathroom, Porky could hear the crowd cheering for the next set. He knew they loved when a ranked player got beaten by someone unranked, someone on the come up. He imagined them all clamoring for blood and his body felt heavy.

He cleaned himself up and stepped out into the crowd with the sole mission of getting black coffee and a banana, his personal hangover cure. He still had a full day of bracket play ahead of him and now he had to make a loser's run, which meant playing several more matches than he'd intended.

"Tough loss!" someone called to him.

Porky ignored him and continued onward, toward the hotel's coffee shop.

In line, he finally checked his phone, but it only made him feel worse. He made the requisite order and ate the rather bruised banana quickly, hardly chewing the moist flesh before swallowing. The coffee was still too hot to drink, so he just inhaled the smell, hoping it would clear his head.

Porky licked the salty moisture from his upper lip and reconsidered all the ways he could have approached the set with Molly. He still couldn't believe she was the same person he'd danced with the night prior. He remembered Dumpster pointing him out at the bar and tried not to feel any ill will about the situation.

I just need to warm up, he thought to himself. If I can find someone to practice with, I can get my hands warm.

The VIP lounge was specifically designed for moments like this — it provided a place to escape from the crowds and focus before your next set. He had thirty minutes still, and would thankfully play offscreen, so he went to the lounge intending only to drink coffee and play against anyone willing, or barring that, the CPU auto-player.

A few players sat on the red VIP sofas, mostly absorbed on their phones. No one said anything when he entered and Porky resigned himself to playing alone, until Mums, looking like someone who had slept a full night, approached him.

"Hey man, you want to warm up?"

Porky felt a wave of gratitude and nodded.

They navigated to the screen where Porky chose his raccoon and Mums chose the rat character. The rat was faster than the other characters, but he didn't have any special attacks aside from biting and 'stealing the cheese,' which was more or less a bomb made of Swiss cheese that was thrown at his opponent. However, the rat was also the most popular character for newbies to play because he was so streamlined and quick. Mums knew Porky would be playing more than one rat that day and was willing to help his friend.

They played evenly, each of them taking a game, before a tournament volunteer alerted Porky that it was time for him to go back down.

"Thanks for the warmup."

He fist-bumped Mums, finished his large coffee, and went back into the melee below.

The rest of his loser's bracket run was a hazy, over-caffeinated blur, as he destroyed rat after rat, another bird, and an opossum. He didn't register the players' names — he could look them up online later, just mechanically fist-bumped and moved on to the next one.

By the end of the day, he'd plowed through his competition to secure a spot in the top eight players who were entering the grand finals. Now, he had to play 'best of five' games for each set.

His first top eight competitor was Flip, a SoCal player who was one of numbChux's friends, they even had the same sponsor. Porky walked on stage; the crowd cheered and jeered in equal measure. He saw several guys up front wearing snouts, which gave him some much-needed confidence. He flexed and growled at the camera; Flip stood, and they shook hands. They were back on either side of two monitors, which blocked their view of one another; behind them was the large projector screen showing their gameplay to the audience.

Porky could hear Gordon's voice booming across mass of humans, but the content was lost in the cacophony. He felt confident, he'd been playing without breaks all day and was ready to take on Flip, who happened to play a rat, and had a reputation as being one of the fastest *Trash Fighters* players.

The first game started off strong: Porky's raccoon got off several 'rabies' attacks before Flip's rat could even respond. But, once the rat was loose on the stage, he ran around so quickly that Porky felt like he was just chasing him. He chose to sit in the center and lure the rat to him, which worked for a minute. Then, faster than he could respond, Flip's rat pushed him off stage and threw a cheese bomb that prevented him from recovering. Now, playing once again from behind, Porky began to feel the same way he had felt that morning. He tuned out the crowd and disregarded his roiling stomach. It was no use; Flip was in his head and the rat was in control of the next game as well. Porky took game three, but ultimately the results were 1-3 in Flip's favor.

Again, he swallowed his pride and stood — he dwarfed Flip entirely, but they hugged and congratulated each other. Flip would move on and Porky was out of the tournament at eighth place. He collected his controller and what was left of his dignity, waved to the crowd and the Twitch camera, then walked out of the auditorium.

"Can we take a photo?" someone asked him.

"No, not right now."

He knew he would catch shit on Twitter, but he had to get out of there.

The casino had no end of bars, so it was easy to find a quiet place to sit and feign interest in sports or video poker while nursing a beer. He consoled himself, he'd earned a high-enough place to earn enough money to make the whole endeavor worthwhile. He hadn't compromised his ranking and his sponsor would be glad enough he'd placed in the top ten. Plus, now he was done, he could relax. He closed his eyes and began to roll his head around, unclenching his shoulders.

"Hey Porks."

Before he opened his eyes, he already knew who it was, "Hey Llama. Or Drama? I'm not sure which is the most fitting."

She laughed. "Can I buy you a beer?"

"You'll have to do better than that."

"A beer and a shot."

He opened his eyes and regarded her. Her eyeliner was smudged from the damp human heat of the crowded venue, but she still looked pretty. She was wearing glasses she hadn't worn the night before, which felt like a year ago now.

"Accepted," he held out his hand and she shook it.

"Can I get two boilermakers?"

The drinks appeared instantly.

"So, how'd you do?"

"Oh, I got kicked into losers immediately after beating you and was swiftly eliminated."

"No epic losers run?"

"I'll leave that to the top players. But I made it to top 64, which isn't bad, considering I didn't think I'd place at all. I might sneak into the next rankings list."

Porky took a long sip of beer. "I have to ask, were you trying to sabotage me last night?"

"What? No, of course not."

"I mean, it worked out pretty well for you."

"It did. But I also didn't know how much you and Dumpster had partied beforehand, at least not until I saw his Instagram story last night and then I felt a little bad."

"So, you just wanted to dance?"

"With you, yeah. I know Dumpster from some of the local tournaments and he told me to 'get over myself' and go talk to you, so I did."

Porky smiled, he felt corny and happy.

"Are you staying in Vegas tonight?" he asked.

"Yeah, I have my hotel for a couple more days."

"Well, what if we showered, god knows I need it, and then went to the *Trash Fighters* after-party together, they rented out one of the rooftop clubs at Caesar's Palace."

"And you want to go together? Like a date?"

"Yes, exactly like that."

Molly tilted her head to one side, she looked adorably owl-like with her glasses and Porky's heart thudded a little in his chest.

"Okay," she replied. "I wasn't planning to go, but I did bring a cute dress that I'd like to take out. Let's do it!"

Porky finished his beer and stood, "Alright! Meet me down here in an hour? They should be almost done by then. We can catch grands, then grab a drink and head over."

Molly stood on her tiptoes and kissed the bottom of his cheek, "See you then!"

Down the corridor, out of their earshot, Flip took a game off Mums, the current number one ranked player, and the crowd erupted into a victorious cheer — another upset! A hundred heads dipped simultaneously to re-live the action, regurgitated now, onto their phones.

Funz0 @funz_0: I was in Vegas and PorkyDig wouldn't even stop to talk to me.

Ed @EddieZoom replying to @funz_0: *what a cuck*

Chuck pulled into a gas station — he'd been driving for hours and needed a break. The flat, endless desert stretched out in front of him and tumbleweeds kept rolling across the highway. The landscape recalled a particular scene in *Red Dead Redemption*.

The gas station door pinged with a soft chime as he entered. Just above the door was a security camera — Chuck stared at it boldly, feeling the safe embrace of anonymity. No one knew he was here. No one cared. He had disappeared.

Well, not entirely. He'd texted his parents that he was taking a vacation, so they knew he was okay. He wasn't trying to go full *Into the Wild* on everyone. Plus, he figured Lois would feed Miss Mittens and she might also be thankful for a break from his late-night gaming.

The cool air blasted him as he opened a refrigerated case to browse energy drinks. The thing was, he didn't even really like energy drinks. His sponsor's own brand stared accusingly at him from the cohort of caffeinated beverages and Chuck shut the case closed. He bought an Arizona iced tea and a bag of Cheez-its instead.

At the checkout, the cashier didn't meet his eyes and simply recited what he owed.

"I need to put twenty dollars on pump three as well," Chuck added.

"Okay."

He paid and went outside to fill his gas tank. One other truck idled near the restrooms and a sedan full of kids was parked at pump one, their harangued-looking father standing over them, cleaning the windshield with a squeegee.

Chuck checked his phone; he'd had it on airplane mode for forty-eight hours and, when he reverted the settings back to normal, every app buzzed so violently with an onslaught of messages that he almost threw it out into the road. He ignored the texts, the Discord messages, and instead searched his web browser for the *Trash Fighters* tournament in Las Vegas.

Some of the winners were unexpected — he knew how much people loved an unexpected upset, especially at a big tournament — it made him thankful he wasn't there.

News alerts chosen by an algorithm that knew his preferred topics popped up: *Where is numbChux?Amateur Reddit Sleuths are on the Case!* followed by *Popular Hot Tub Streamer, Anthem, is Back in Action After On-Stream Accident* and several e-sports articles about all of the Vegas events.

The gas pump clicked. Chuck put his phone on 'do not disturb' and removed Discord from his phone. Back inside the car, he opened his snacks; the tart lemon sweetness of the tea was pleasant. Chuck input GPS coordinates into his phone's map application, watching as the line appeared that would take him the rest of the way to the ocean.

1

Anthem had purchased the inflatable hot tub off Amazon and illuminated it with purple and blue Christmas lights. In the background she strung a garland of silver blue strands of paper like you might see at a pool-themed birthday party and arranged a couple of fake palm trees. In the hot tub itself, she placed a small inflatable raft that held a pink rubber ducky and several hard seltzers. It was more like a lukewarm tub, but that wasn't really the point.

Her Twitch stream's lead moderator messaged her in their private Discord thread: *Ready to go live?*

Almost, she typed back.

Tonight, she wore a bright red wig that, along with her purple bikini, gave off a little mermaid in the grotto feeling she hoped would attract new viewers. The camera was angled downward to give her breasts more prominence. She'd attached sparkling jewels around her eyes and they glittered like iridescent fish scales. Three monitors faced her, one had chat, the other was for anything she may need to look up on screen, and the third showed her stream, which was in preview mode right now. The preview screen mirrored her face back to herself and the familiar performance anxiety settled into her stomach. Anthem used the preview screen to adjust her wig and bikini top before messaging her moderator.

Okay, put up the waiting image with a countdown for viewers. Let's double-check and make sure everyone is ready to moderate the chat. Remember, any offensive language gets a 2-hour ban. We aren't doing warnings tonight.

She received a series of thumbs up emojis blinking in quick yellow succession from the chat mods on duty for her that evening.

Anthem watched the stream go live; her camera remained off for now. She could already see people joining the chat and saying hi, some of the long-tern subscribers were even greeting each other. Anthem was gratified knowing that she was the reason these people connected. *And, besides, it was better than stripping*, she thought. She could sit in a hot tub in her own home and make just as much money in one evening.

She posted a link to her Twitch stream on Twitter with the message: *Going live now!* accompanied by a kiss emoji.

Lfg! she typed into Discord.

She turned on the copious ring lights surrounding the pool, adjusted her microphone, and when she pressed 'start streaming' her capped-tooth smile was already plastered on for the camera.

"Hi everyone, I hope y'all are having a good evening."

She watched the chat on her monitor respond with fire and heart emojis.

"I just thought we could hang out tonight and chat. How does that sound? I'll be doing some sub goals and playing the ukulele too."

She pulled a ukulele from offscreen and began strumming it.

"What do you say, five subs for a song?"

Quickly, five new subscriptions came through and her stream automatically played a quick GIF of her blowing a kiss in the corner of the screen as a 'thank you' response.

"Alright, alright! I just learned this one, so be kind."

Anthem began to strum the opening chords of "Over the Rainbow" and hummed along with the opening bars before fully committing her voice to the song. Playing music always transported her and made her feel like what she was doing was much larger and more closely tied to her creativity.

As she sang, she heard the sub counter ding and she tried to resist the urge to tally up the money she was making. When the song ended, she leaned forward to check the chat and began responding to some of their comments in a bizarre one-sided conversation that constituted many of her 'just chatting' streams.

"Aw thanks, y'all! Sure, I'll play again later. Let me know if you have any requests, hit !ukelele to see the list of songs I know. Cheers? Is it already time for a cheers? Well, alright then. How about a sub, and then we can cheers to it?"

The sub counter dinged.

Anthem pulled a small, inflated raft over to her and opened one of the pre-prepped hard seltzers.

"Cheers to the subs! What else should we cheers to? My chest? Calm down. The wig? Alright, I'll pour one out for her hard work this evening."

She raised the hard seltzer toward the camera in hearty false camaraderie.

A message came through that tagged her: This is the downfall of streaming. Then another: Not only is she boring, she's ugly too. And: If a guy did this, he'd be banned so fast.

The messages disappeared as quickly as they arrived, Anthem knew her mods were probably working overtime, but her smile didn't falter and she took another sip of her drink.

"What's everyone else drinking tonight? Whiskey on the rocks, oh that's too strong for me. Beer, beer, yeah okay, beer seems to be the popular choice. A Long Island Iced Tea? Where are you, sir? Do you make those at home? That is a dangerous skill to have!"

She finished her drink and placed the empty can back on her little raft.

"Have y'all met Ducky yet? He's my new toy."

She placed the rubber duck in the water and gave him a little push.

"He's a little shy though and needs some encouragement."

She heard another sub ding in, and then a donation that automatically played a computerized voice over: *Let's gooooo, Ducky!*

"Let's see if I can catch him!"

Anthem lowered her shoulders under the water and began to swim, although it was more a kneeling and flapping of her arms in the shallow hot tub. She put on a performative predatory bit as she stalked toward the neon pink duck. Then, in one quick motion she scooped the duck up between her breasts who, when she emerged, was riding high on her chest like a tightrope walker.

"Got him!"

She bounced a little, glistening in the lighting she'd set up for explicitly this purpose.

"Quack quack! Alright Ducky, that's enough. Get out of here."

She placed the rubber duck back in the pool and thought to herself that no one would ever know how long she had practiced that little stunt, proving to herself that it could ever look sexy. Her efforts appeared to be worth it though, as she'd gained a few subs.

"Cheers to Ducky!"

She opened another hard seltzer and grabbed a waterproof marker from the small floating raft and its hidden trove of props. "Okay, the next sub gets to choose what I write on me, and where."

Three subscriptions came in rapidly and her mod typed out a winner in the chat: **@MarkyArt**.

"Alright, MarkyArt, name your prize! Nothing on the face though."

> »   MarkyArt: Write Mark with a heart below your clavicle.

Anthem obliged and wrote his name with a heart right above her own.

This went on for a while, she had to cap it when her more accessible body parts were completely covered in writing. She looked like a desk at the back of the classroom with all manner of names carved into it. Now, the trick was, she had to stay on a little longer so those people who paid for the privilege of her skin could feel as though they'd truly gotten their money's worth. It was just like lingering in the VIP suite of a strip club — you had to leave before they got bored, while their interest was still piqued enough to come back next week.

Her mod messaged her in Discord, Let's do another twenty minutes and call it.

Anthem leaned forward to type a message to the moderators and her knee lost purchase, her body slipped forward. The bottom of the hot tub was slick from the glitter body oil she'd put on before the stream. Her hand grabbed at the tray that held her keyboard, attached to the microphone stand. Panicking, she pulled herself a little too hard and the whole thing came tumbling toward her. The inflatable hot tub lit up brightly for a moment, then everything went black.

The stream was still technically running in the now offline darkness. The stream feed had died, and the viewers in chat were having apoplectic attacks. Some were howling for confirmation that Anthem was safe, some were laughing and thought it served her right, and others were only angry because that was their base function on the internet.

Mods messaged Anthem's private Discord nonstop, but there were no longer any pings in her dark, silent room, she could no longer hear anything at all. Finally, one of Anthem's moderators called the police and asked them to respond to her address. There was nothing to do but turn off the stream and wait.

The EMT workers found her lying half in the hot tub still, her wig askew, and fully clad in her little mermaid bikini — she looked like a sea nymph who'd accidentally made it ashore, but she was completely unconscious. They discerned a pulse and hypothesized mild electrocution. She didn't wake up during the ambulance ride when, strapped to a gurney, one of the EMT workers took a surreptitious photo of her; he recognized her face from the Top Streamers page of Twitch.

Anthem finally awoke a few hours later in the hospital. She took in her surroundings and pieced together that she'd been in some way injured. She didn't question, in the moment, how she'd ended up in the hospital, but simply accepted it. Her limbs tingled and her right shoulder hurt quite badly, but she was able to shrug it upwards, relieved it wasn't broken or dislocated. She rolled over to her left side, nursing her right, and recognized the figure of a short, stocky woman with steel grey hair piled on top of her head.

"Mama?"

The woman turned to face her. She was a shadowy silhouette, backlit by the hospital's window.

"Yes. Natalie Anne? Can you hear me?"

Her mother's presence somehow seemed the most far-fetched part of this whole experience.

"I can hear you, Mama."

"You were electrocuted being a whore on video, just so you know. They said you're gonna be fine, but they called me anyway."

"Oh."

She remembered it all now, the tumble forward and her panic, then a bright white light before the darkness. Anthem's first thought was that it would affect her subscribers. No one wanted to see a messy hot tub stream. But on the other hand, they may have felt enough pity to want to support her further. Her mods would be disappointed; they kept telling her not to drink on stream. The hard seltzers, and the shots of vodka beforehand, just made everything a little easier. In the last moment before she'd slipped, she'd seen her mother's disapproving face and felt the shadow of shame that permeated everything she did. She looked down, though her fish scales had fallen off, the faded marker remnants twined around her arms like henna.

"I hope you learned your lesson. The devil's work is all you're doing. You didn't learn anything from your aunt Martha's mistake, running herself ragged for men until one of them killed her. Is that what you want for yourself? Martha never got right with the Lord and that was her folly. It will be your folly too."

Anthem remembered Aunt Martha in her childhood. She had looked up to her with her big orange hair and tight Wrangler jeans. Martha snuck Anthem candies from her purse when her mother wasn't looking since she wasn't allowed to have sugar. Her funeral was the first Anthem had experienced as a child and the smell of graveside lilies still made her nauseous.

But here, in this present moment, all she wanted was for her mother to pet her head and tell her it would be all right. Her mother was not one to show outward affection. 'My love is between me and the Lord,' she always said. Martha, on the other hand, was free with her affection and often kissed Anthem on the head. Why had this woman driven an hour from the trailer park outside Tacoma just to yell at her? Why are you here at all, she wanted to ask, why can't you just love me?

"Maybe now you'll come to Jesus," her mother muttered, turning back to the window.

That was it, Anthem decided. That's what she would do.

"But mama," she began, "I did see Jesus."

"Don't fool around with the Lord," her mother said sharply, her tongue still lashed Anthem like a viper's.

"I'm not, I swear. Right before everything went dark, the last thing I remember was a bright white light and then I saw someone's face. I knew they were going to keep me safe, so I wasn't worried. He even brought you here, isn't that right?"

Her mother looked down at her hands, "It's true. I felt a powerful calling to be here for you."

"You see?"

"If you had a visitation, he would've said something to you," her mother turned toward her.

"He just smiled at me, everything was bright and I just knew I'd be okay," Anthem pressed on, straining to see the other woman's reaction in the fluorescent lighting.

The hard line of her mother's mouth wavered a little and she stared at Anthem as though she wanted to see clear through her to the other side, like she wanted Anthem to become as transparent as an onion skin and reveal all of her secrets. Unfortunately, her daughter was still flesh and blood and yielded nothing but a pensive face, illuminated by the small window in the white hospital room.

"I think..." Anthem tried out her new idea, "I want to devote my life to Jesus."

"What do you mean?"

"I think I could help people."

"What people?"

"Just people, you know, like someone who goes on a mission trip, only I'd be doing it online."

"You want to be a pastor?"

"More like a life coach, or a youth leader."

"You've gotta prove to Jesus that you're worthy of a vocation like that. Just because he came to you in a vision doesn't mean you've earned his love."

"Mama," Anthem began in the calm, neutral voice she reserved for assholes who tried to get too handsy at the strip club, "Jesus is only love. You don't have to earn it."

Her mother's eyes narrowed to dark slits and she reeled back to give a withering retort, that died on her lips as the doctor entered and exclaimed, "You're awake, welcome back!"

He began to check numbers, prodding at Anthem and asking questions.

"You seem to be fine, everything we've checked is perfectly normal. We do want to keep you tonight for observation, but tomorrow you'll be able to go home. I'd just recommend taking it easy for a few days. Oh," he gestured toward her side table upon which was a glass of water and, in the drawer underneath, a Bible, a fact that Anthem knew although she couldn't see it, "The EMTs grabbed your cell phone and wallet, they're in the drawer. Just in case you needed to get in touch with anyone else."

"Thank you, doctor," she blinked her large doll-like eyes at him and watched him falter just a moment over his words.

"Um, well, alright, and have a good night. And ma'am, visiting hours are almost over."

"I was about to leave anyway."

Her mother gathered her things and followed the doctor toward the door, turning back to add, "You should spend tonight praying to the Lord."

"Of course, I'll thank him for giving me a second chance to walk on the earth in his shadow."

Her mother grimaced and left the room, closing the door behind her.

Alone, the desire to laugh bubbled up inside Anthem's chest. This had been one of the most ridiculous days of her life. Her first thought was to message her mods and tell them she was okay, but it felt like a monumental effort. She knew a clip of her falling was most likely already being replayed by strangers all over the internet. Instead of engaging in that mess, she ignored all the notifications on her phone and opened her Notes app where she began writing up a new set of rules for herself.

Re-brand.

1. *Change stream name?*
2. *Keep a 'spiritual' angle*
3. *Merchandise?*
4. *Ukelele for Christianity*
5. *No more hot tub stream*
6. *Switch to playing Call of Duty*
7. *Community? TikTok? YouTube?*
8. *Life-coaching should be the ultimate goal*
9. *Need a website*

Anthem lay back on the flat, pastel blue hospital pillow and sighed. No one had thought to bring her any clothes, so she was forced to continue wearing the hospital gown which barely reached her knees and didn't provide anything in the way of comfort or warmth. She pulled the thin blanket up to her chest and thought about her mother and Martha taking her to Cowboy Church.

The church itself was more like a white circus tent; it reminded Anthem now of revival preachers in the South. Inside, people sat on hay bales, looking expectantly toward a wooden stage that was sometimes used for cattle auctioneering. A man in pressed and creased jeans, a pearl snap button-down shirt, cowboy boots and an accompanying cowboy hat stood, smiling benevolently at anyone who entered. Anthem remembered being disappointed there was no bloody depiction of Christ looking down over them, there were no icons at all, aside from this carefully starched man.

They took a seat on one of the middle hay bales, Anthem sat in between her mother and aunt and began scooting around, unable to get comfortable on the scratchy seat.

"Stop squirming," her mother hissed.

Martha looked down at her and winked.

Anthem tried to rearrange herself in a way that would allow her legs to stop itching without further annoying her mother.

"Welcome to all the sheep of this here flock! Welcome," the man intoned.

He began speaking about covetousness, something Anthem didn't really understand at the time, using the example of a man coveting another man's tractor.

"Now, I know Mister Smathers over here, he may have the best darn John Deere in the county, but that doesn't give me any right to want it for myself."

Anthem tried not to fall asleep and stabbed herself in the thigh with a sharp piece of hay whenever boredom threatened to close her eyes.

"It's time for the baptismal. Who here is new to our church?"

Anthem's mother raised her hand and forcibly raised Anthem's.

"Welcome," his attention was only on them now. "And who here would like to come forward and accept Jesus into their heart?"

Anthem's mother was standing before anyone could protest and dragging Anthem forward with her, pieces of hay falling off her cotton dress as they approached the wooden platform. Once they'd reached the front, she looked out at the other people still seated; their placid faces looked sedated, though a few older women in the front row smiled encouragingly.

The man led Anthem to a horse's trough filled with water.

"Are you ready to accept Jesus Christ as your Lord and Savior?"

Her mother nudged her hard in the ribs and Anthem spat out, "Yes, I am."

They helped her take off her shoes and stand in the horse trough. The water was freezing cold, as though it had been left out overnight in the frost. She lowered herself down, teeth chattering, and listened as the man said some sort of prayer.

"Lord Jesus Christ has freed you from sin, given you a new birth by water, and you will emerge cleansed and welcomed as a sheep in Jesus's flock."

With that, he pressed her head underneath the water, one hand at the base of her neck and the other on her forehead. When she emerged, gasping, Anthem didn't feel reborn, but angry as a wet cat. She hissed and spat while the onlookers applauded and the man with the cowboy hat looked pleased with himself, calling her his lamb. Her wet dress clung to her thin, adolescent body and she forced a smile. Her mother, looming over her, dragged Anthem, sodden, back to her seat on the hay bale. Her mother hadn't brought her an extra set of clothes then either and made her ride in the back of their truck so as not to get the upholstery wet on the ride home.

It didn't actually take much maneuvering to rebrand — Anthem decided to keep her screen name and people were so concerned about her that, when she went live, they tuned in immediately. She'd become a viral story, and her brief absence allowed the initial story to grow. During her time away, she bought a new wardrobe of primarily athleisure in neutral tones and wore more modest clothing on her stream, large sweaters over bike shorts.

She played *Call of Duty*, which attracted some of the more conservative crowd when she hit the streaming stats leaderboard. The problem was it was mostly men, so she eventually exchanged *CoD* for *Animal Crossing*, she said she wanted to inspire others to find a meditative state within gaming rather than promote violence. She still played the ukulele on stream but moved her lyrical focus to devotional songs.

Her moderators all left, they weren't on board with the new version of Anthem even with the almost dying part, but they were easy enough to replace. To capture a younger female audience, she expanded to YouTube and TikTok where she began posting videos about manifestation and using journaling as a tool to bring powerful good into your life. She posted her cozy gaming setup replete with candles and fresh flowers and all the aesthetic elements of the divine feminine.

She worked with a graphic designer to create a daily affirmation journal and sold it through her website and on Amazon. She shared her story about the bright light and how she knew she wanted to do something different with her life. Her journal was listed on several social media influencer gift guides. Anthem watched her TikTok follower count climb, her YouTube videos were some of the most watched in their categories, and people were sharing unprompted testimonials of how her journal had helped them. She knew a book deal was close at hand.

Still, the comments on YouTube were often a duality of disbelievers and defenders:

> » This rebrand is so inauthentic.
>   She was just showing her tits
>   all over stream a few weeks ago.
> » People can change.
> » She's giving off spiritual LA
>   crystal charger vibes.
> » She had a near death experience.

» So she says.
» Yeah. No one knows what really
  happened.

And they were right, they would never really know.

Her YouTube page wasn't meant to pop off the way it did. She'd intended it to be a hobby, a place to connect with other like-minded people, other history buffs. In her downtime, Astrid watched video after video discussing humanity's cultural oddities, their wars, their glorious pasts in the low light of her studio apartment in a city where she was pursuing a graduate degree in Medieval Studies but was yet to make any friends.

Her days consisted of attending classes titled *Problems in Church History 800-1500* and *Art and Race in Medieval Europe*, then spending hours in the library reading about dead people. She sat in the silence, opening thick books to expose illuminated manuscripts bereft of their gold leaf — the solitude also caused her to occasionally question what she was doing with her life. Maybe she should be living more kinetically, less inside herself. Her body felt like a flesh prison at times that held only her beating heart and the whirling, anxious knowledge stored inside her mind. If she closed her eyes, she could hear it all buzzing inside her ears; it was then that she longed for the cool silence of the catacombs she'd never visited but could imagine fully.

At night she watched videos online, meandering mini-documentaries on YouTube where people explored abandoned buildings and shared the forgotten history of their towns. Sometimes she watched true crime videos, which were most often young women exploring theories around grisly murders, posting crime scene photos; some even did their makeup while their pre-recorded voiceover told the viewer about a husband who'd taken the kitchen scissors to his wife. Like any aspiring Medievalist, Astrid appreciated the macabre, the confrontation with death. Mostly, these videos dulled the noise inside her own head, especially in the early morning hours when sleep often eluded her.

She lived in a small town, but one with history concealed around every corner. It felt wrong to study Medieval history while living in a town where the oldest building only dated back to the eighteenth century. Still, inspired by the YouTubers, she decided she needed to get outside more and garner a feel for the place. She kept an eye out for historical plaques and stopped to read all of them.

When Astrid found the cemetery in her wanderings, it felt like a godsend. The great oak trees, only just changing color in anticipation of the fall, created a private border that made her feel as though she'd stepped backward in time. Ancient-looking headstones were covered in moss, and she strained to make out some of the names hidden underneath. She walked slowly through the grounds and took a few pictures of particularly worn-out headstones with her phone. At first, she felt a sort of hesitancy in invading their privacy, but she soon gave that up and crouched over the graves in her black Chelsea boots and long skirt, touching the granite and cement structures gingerly with her long fingers. The sound of her fingernails scraping against the rock was the only noise aside from a few songbirds.

It didn't take much effort to find the cemetery's public record book online and begin to look up the names. She clarified a few she couldn't make out in her photos. Then, she began to hunt around. Her specialty was research and she quickly compiled a composite image of the graveyard's inhabitants.

Astrid returned to the cemetery a few times before finally deciding to film a YouTube video, her first. She used her phone to film the graves, mostly those in disrepair, showing her hands with their chipped black nail polish brushing aside spiderwebs and moss. Her soft voice narrated the names she read off dilapidated tombstones and what she'd learned of the cemetery from the local record books. She showed a cobbler's grave with an etching of a shoe. She explained the importance of symbolism on headstones throughout the ages.

Finally, she came to the reason she'd decided to make the video. The grave of a young woman, Mary Addler, buried under a tombstone with an etching of an angel crying, the angel's hands clasped a single rose. Her death was in 1792, a date Astrid knew felt impossibly buried in the past to most people.

"Mary Addler was the first victim of the man who would go on to be known as the Virgin Killer. He only killed young women and girls, often before their eighteenth birthdays, always leaving their bodies on public display. At first, it was thought to be the work of an entire cult, Satanists, some kind of punishment laid upon the town by a holy order, by God himself. Only it was a single man who traveled up and down the East Coast for much of the decade leaving a trail of bloodied nightdresses in his wake."

Astrid kept her voice soft as she narrated. She had planned her visit to the cemetery to coincide with golden hour and the soft light created sunbeams that she filtered through her phone's lens. The fiery red and orange of the oak trees cast a romantic yet grim backdrop. As the sun set, she panned across the dim expanse, allowing lens flares to pop up in the right corner of her recording, before finally focusing on the victim's tombstone one last time.

"The grave of Mary Addler has important symbolism. The crying angel obviously represents her innocence, the tragedy of a life ended in youth and in such a gruesome manner. The angel is also clutching a rose which often symbolizes beauty, sometimes courage, both attributes we can give to Mary Addler, whose only photograph is one of youthful beauty."

Later, when Astrid was at home editing the video, she used this pause at the end to show an image of Mary Addler in a high-necked dress, looking severe for her young age, but certainly one could imagine the blush of her cheeks, the soft golden curls that escaped from her tied back hair. As the image faded, Astrid read, in a voice barely above a whisper, the newspaper clipping about Mary Addler's tragic demise.

Ultimately, the graveyard video project distracted her for the couple of days leading up to her *Manuscript Studies* final exam. She felt proud of her amateur video, that she'd been able to share her research and make it look somewhat artistic. Maybe all those art history classes hadn't been entirely for nothing. She didn't even hate how her voice sounded. Right before she had to submit work for her finals, Astrid uploaded her first video to YouTube. In the description, she added MLA-formatted citations, including information about the local record books and where she'd found the article. She pressed 'upload,' and did not think about YouTube again until after her exams and essays had all been submitted.

In the in-between, people found her video and the true crime community catapulted Astrid into the virtual spotlight. One influencer called her a 'micro-documentarian' and insisted she capture additional content. People in the comments agreed they were absolutely dying for her ASMR voice and artsy visuals.

When Astrid opened her YouTube page a couple of weeks later, intending only to watch a video to quiet her mind in the wake of her first semester ending, she saw all the comments on her own video that had flooded in:

> » I'd listen to her read anything. Love a sad girl narrating a tragedy.
>> » Replying: Choke me, sad girl.
> » Fix ur nail polish grl.
> » What's the angle here? There's no angle so, ergo, it cannot be a documentary.
>> » Replying: She never said it was a documentary. Where did she say it was a documentary?
> » Mary Addler's archived death notice: link. She didn't even mention they never caught the killer!! Who was he?
>> » Replying: Sleuths, get to work!
> » Where's the next video?
> » Shes fr uggo, y no face?
> » This right here, this is what's wrong with society.

There was no context to the last comment, was Astrid contributing to the downfall of society, or was it unnamed serial killers? She felt overwhelmed by the interest, the demands, but disgusted by some of the other comments people felt comfortable writing when hidden by the anonymous curtain of the internet. She turned off notifications and switched over to Netflix.

One morning, the sky stretched itself like a large aquamarine canvas in front of her window, and Astrid noticed the trees were beginning now to lose their leaves. It felt like an invitation, and she walked to the university's library to delve further into researching the Virgin Killer.

She explored the microfiche selection and read newspaper articles through the viewer, black and white images modernity had forgotten about. As the story was both gruesome and punchy, the papers of the time spent a considerable amount of ink on the whole thing. She took photos and made printouts when she could, eventually piecing together that another victim was buried in a cemetery only a few towns over. Astrid reasoned that she could road trip there and create another video without much fuss.

The next day she warmed up her car, cold from disuse, and loaded up a tote bag with printed research, a half-formed script, and copious car snacks. It hadn't yet begun to snow, but people in town kept talking about it as an inevitability. Astrid had never lived anywhere with snow before and she regarded the natural phenomenon with a healthy amount of fear.

It won't snow on the trip, she assured herself as she pulled the car out onto the highway, its transmission wheezing a little.

The cemetery, when she reached it, was smaller and more densely packed than the one in her town. The grave of Rebecca Astore was easy to find. Astrid touched the gravestone and noticed that her nail polish was again chipped. Well, that can be my signature thing, she thought.

Because this graveyard was also significantly more planted, shadows cast from the thin trees created an eerie effect on the headstones and Astrid thought it would be the perfect time to begin filming. She placed her script on the ground next to her and began narrating the news story about Rebecca Astore's grisly murder, her body left in a tree outside her family home to be found by her parents upon their return from town.

She filmed several long shots of the cemetery, making sure to capture the gentle rippling branches of the trees, their dark and spindly arms reaching up toward an unbearably clear sky.

Astrid wondered what the weather was like on Rebecca's last day. Had she stepped outside in this same small town and looked up at the same sky? Had the trees appeared ominous to her?

Later that evening, she uploaded the video after she'd added photos of newspaper articles and a dappled lighting filter. She closed her laptop and made herself a cup of herbal tea. That night, Astrid dreamed only bloody nightmares of Mary and Rebecca — she dreamed of a white dress blowing in the wind against a cloudless sky, a faceless woman turned away from her as the white dress became slowly drenched in red as though steeped in a tea cup of blood.

The next morning, comments had already begun to roll in:

> » Who is interested in this stuff?
>> » Replying: I come to feed my own morbid curiosity, but stay for the education
>> » Replying: Twisted people, mostly women
> » I've had to rewatch this 5x because her voice is so relaxing, I could listen to this woman read cereal boxes!
>> » Replying: Big Mooooood
>> » Replying: I watched this as I fell asleep last night, like it was a fucked-up bedtime story
> » I wonder what the Virgin Killer's zodiac sign was. Both Mary and Rebecca are Sags.
> » Does anyone else think this is disrespectful to the victims' families?

» Replying: If they even
  have any living relatives.

Astrid made a couple more research-based videos over her long winter break, even revisiting the initial cemetery to discuss some of the other underground inhabitants. People couldn't get enough of them and were re-sharing clips of them on TikTok as well. Astrid had not yet shown her face to the camera, but no one really seemed to mind.

She walked through her town's graveyard with confidence now, sometimes not to film, but to read a book on the stone bench. She enjoyed the quiet, the birds and squirrels. It still hadn't snowed.

On one such afternoon, Astrid sensed someone else in the graveyard with her; she assumed tourists and did not look up from her book. She overheard a rushed conversation accompanied by a quick rustling of leaves and finally raised her head. Two figures in dark overcoats stared back at her. Her first instinct was to wave and acknowledge their shared humanity, then she realized they might be in mourning, and kept her hand in her lap. One of the figures appeared to be aiming their cell phone at her, maybe checking a map, but they hadn't made any moves. Astrid felt a skin-prickling discomfort and left her bench to walk toward the cemetery's exit.

Although she felt certain the graveyard tourists were harmless, she did sometimes feel watched. She started putting a piece of tape over the camera on her laptop and observing the way a green light shone on her phone to indicate she'd activated the camera. When her fingers were swooshing over an app where endless videos played on demand, no need to press anything, she'd catch someone's eyes staring back out at her, only to realize it was a targeted advertisement. The digital eyes were blind to her own.

Eventually, she went back to the graveyard and filmed for another short video. People had begun adding hashtags to her uploads: cottagecore, moonaesthetic, romanticizeyourdeath. Now that classes were starting back up, she wouldn't have as much time to engage online. *Although maybe that was a good thing*, she thought to herself as she took video of her feet crunching in the fresh fallen snow.

A few days later, Astrid sat in the back of her *Byzantine Arts and Architecture* lecture taking copious notes. She was utterly engrossed in the mosaics, frescoes, and ivory carvings of Byzantium, oblivious to the hurriedly scratching pens of those around her, focused only on the deep lull of her professor's voice as he described the materials most often used in frescoes of the time.

The lecture concluded and Astrid struggled to stuff her tote bag with an array of study materials. Her professor bid her goodbye and strode off to his office hours. It was only then that Astrid clocked another person still in the small classroom with her.

"Hey," a male voice greeted her.

She looked up. He was wearing a navy blue peacoat and his dark blonde hair was mussed in a way that wasn't unattractive.

"Hi."

"I keep seeing you around."

He bared his eye teeth in a half smile.

"Oh?" she asked.

She finished packing up her things and stood to face him.

"I wanted to ask your name."

"Astrid."

"You have the posture of a Norse goddess."

Astrid's shoulders sank under the weight of his compliment.

"I'm Ryan."

"Well, nice to meet you. I have to go, I have another class," she lied.

"Nice to meet you too, *Astrid*," he called to her retreating back.

Something about Ryan had put her on edge and Astrid made a bee-line for the graveyard. She longed for the hush of the snowy tombs and the exaggerated puff of her frozen breath in front of her.

She walked quickly and without looking over her shoulder, gripping the tote bag to her side. At the stone gates of the graveyard, Astrid noticed someone had cleared the snow off the path.

Just a quick pass, a slow walk, she told herself, just to calm me down.

Her extremities cooled quickly now that she'd left the close warmth of her classroom and she walked more slowly, deepening her breath. She closed her eyes and turned her face toward the weak winter sun. The path ended after a u-shaped bend through the cemetery's center and Astrid walked out the gate again, feeling rejuvenated.

A flash of darkness in her periphery drew Astrid's attention to a copse of trees near the entrance, adjacent to where she was now exiting.

You're imagining things again, she assured herself. She turned toward her apartment and her inner attention to broken pottery along the walls of Constantinople. She opened her apartment's iron gate and locked it behind her. Once upstairs, she put the tea kettle on and booted up her laptop to work on her research, thankful for JSTOR access and for her landlord finally turning on the building's heat.

The kettle whistled and Astrid poured the water over an Earl Grey tea bag which she garnished with a lemon wedge and spoonful of honey. She carried the steamy mug to the window, imagining herself in a cozy holiday movie. Down by the streetlamp, in the white light of the afternoon, she saw a man looking up at her window. They were too far apart to make eye contact, maybe he couldn't see her at all, but she recognized that dark peacoat, the mussed hair, and quickly stepped to the side of the window.

She splashed boiling tea on her hand and stifled a cry.

How did he find where I lived? What does he want? The panicked thoughts streamed past her eyes like movie credits.

When she gathered the courage to peer out the window again, she could only see boot tracks in the snow and a slightly deeper indention from where he had been standing.

At least I didn't imagine it, she thought, though it didn't feel particularly reassuring in that moment. And now her tea had gone cold.

She reheated the kettle and tried again. This time, rather than researching for class, she searched for herself on Google. She looked up her YouTube screen name first. She'd used her own name, sans last name, but there was not exactly an overabundance of Astrid's in general. She had to navigate through several pages before landing on a Reddit sub called *Get Off My Social Media.*

There were posts upon posts documenting several years' worth of influencer posts and commentary on their social lives, their personal decisions. The threads were just the titles of their social media accounts, so people knew where to comment with their judgements. Astrid clicked on some of the top threads for influencers named LindyHop and LocoCocoLemon.

LindyHop / @lindyhopper

> » Why does this girl always look like
>   she needs to bathe? Can someone make
>   soap a trending TikTok topic so this
>   girl will take a shower.
> » I always take one look at her videos
>   and have to slide on outta there.
>   Greaseball, gross.

LocoCocoLemon / @lococolemon

> » Why is this woman always on my fyp?
>   She seems like she's suddenly
>   everywhere, but she dresses like
>   every other girl in NYC who quit
>   their job mid-recession to become a
>   fashion influencer. Her videos are
>   just boilerplate trend salad pulled
>   from what's already all over TikTok.
>   You aren't even Gen-Z! Stop dressing
>   like a teenager!
> » I hate her.
> » WHY does she keep getting
>   sponsorships? She's a 30-something
>   wannabe.

Astrid's recoiled from the harsh anonymous comments. A moment ago, she hadn't even known a place like this existed, a cesspool of shitposting that primarily sought to be cruel. There were a few positive comments here and there and some of the YouTubers especially were beloved. She landed upon a few positive comments in other threads.

> » I love that it showed how to do
>   a winged eyeliner without an eye
>   pencil. So helpful!
> » I can actually watch the
>   sorority rush videos on TikTok
>   for hours. As a former sorority

> girl it really feels
> authentic.
» Half of them look like fake ass
> Dolly Partons though.

The reason her Google search had led her here was discovered only halfway down the first page. The most recent comment was from today.

Astrid Graves / @astridgraves_

» I just found this YouTube
> channel and I am literally
> obsessed! Any other true crime
> fans out there? What do y'all
> think?
» I love how well-researched her
> videos are.
» They feel weirdly cozy. Like I
> should be watching them in front
> of a fire with a cup of cocoa.
> Which is kind of creepy I guess.

Astrid clicked through five pages of comments about her. After her third or fourth video people began to complain.

> » Why doesn't she ever show her
> face? It's weird.
> » Maybe she wants to keep some of
> the anonymity. She's focusing on
> the victims and the scenery and
> providing us with a mental
> escape. Maybe she feels like her
> face would distract from the
> artistic element.
> » She's probably not pretty enough
> for the camera. Maybe her face
> would break that shit.

Astrid noted that this comment had been downvoted quite a bit.

> » Has anyone pinpointed the graveyard yet? I know there was discussion about where it could be.
> » Connecticut, for sure.
> » So, she probably goes to school out there. She mentioned her studies in the second video. Anyone know an Astrid? Lol, jk (sort of).
> » I found her. DM me for details.

Astrid's breath caught in her throat. The username who claimed to have found her was @FriedPlasticToaster. She clicked on the profile and only saw their replies to the thread about herself and a few other influencers. Further down, she found the same user had commented in a thread on muscle cars and another in a blocked group called 'Men About Town.'

She searched for the same username on Instagram and got a match. The account was private, but if she squinted her eyes, she could just make out his mussed blonde hair offset against the blue sky in the circular profile picture.

Pickleball Court Open

Hours: 8am – 6pm, or sunset, whichever comes first.

Posted Rules:
— Green rackets only
— Observe standard pickleball court courtesies
— Singles play only on Court A, doubles play allowed on Courts B & C
— No coaching or tournaments without prior approval, applications must be made fourteen days in advance of event at the city office
— No player may utilize the court for financial gain or monetary enterprise
— Playing on the courts without athletic shoes is forbidden
— No tennis on pickleball courts
— Be respectful of neighbors
— No children or dogs
— No bicycles, skateboards, roller-skates or rollerblades
— Food and drink are discouraged
— Only one ball in play at a time, three balls total on court
— Wait until other players have completed their time and exited the court before entering
— Whenever players are waiting, all players must vacate courts after playing fifteen minutes, unless you've made a reservation, then you may have the court for one hour
— Players waiting to use the court must indicate in some clear way they are in fact waiting
— Reservations are non-transferrable
— There will be no refunds for any reservations

Handmade Sign Affixed Underneath:
OBEY QUIET HOURS!!

Tennis Court Open

Hours: 8am - 6pm

Posted Rules:
— DO NOT PLAY PICKLEBALL ON THIS COURT!

There were pickleball players on the tennis courts again — despite all the signs, some of which Lois had put up personally. She could hear the pop-pop of their plastic rackets and closed her curtain with a grimace.

Lois lived across the walking path from the tennis courts, and for years people had come to play tennis there. All manner of people — kids with their expensive private coaches, senior citizens trying to stay active, couples who prided themselves on an early morning game before biking to work. Lois herself played doubles tennis with her girlfriends bi-monthly. She didn't want to rate herself among the striving senior citizens, but she supposed that's where other people might put them.

Recently, the city had taken over two of the tennis courts and transformed them into pickleball courts.

"What the hell is pickleball?" She asked one of the other neighbors.

"It's like ping pong or badminton meets tennis."

Lois didn't like that one bit.

Now that the courts were installed, it was the endless pop-pop from eight in the morning onward until dusk, and often beyond. The courts didn't have enough lighting to play safely after dark, but Lois caught people wearing headlamps, lit up like frantic cyclopes in the dense darkness.

Pickleball seemed to be especially popular among the college students of their town. Shining with youth and that devil-may-care attitude Lois hated, they always ignored the signs, sometimes they even took selfies in front of them, angling their broad, tanned faces toward the sun. She thought in general they were all too loud, lacked respect, and crowded up the good coffee spots with their laptops — there was nowhere to just sit and read the paper.

Lois made an exception for her young neighbor, Chuck. He was a sweet boy and sometimes brought up her mail. She'd only called the landlord that one time because he'd kept shouting expletives and she could hear them through the wall, words Lois herself would never repeat. He'd apologized the next day with flowers and a box of the truffle chocolates Lois liked. She invited him in for coffee and they sat together at her table; he explained that he played video games for a living. Lois didn't understand how such a thing was possible, but Chuck assured her it was. He said he would soundproof the walls, an assurance Lois privately doubted. Though he *had* been quiet the last few days, she hadn't seen his car in the parking lot and assumed he'd taken off to one of his many tournaments.

Lois also didn't trust the internet since she had gotten a virus several years before on her desktop computer from playing FarmVille. She still checked Facebook every once in a while, but she didn't *trust* it. There was a difference.

After seeing the newest pickleball signs going up, she gave in and decided to log on to her ancient computer and check out the local, online community groups to see if there was any information on the phenomenon. A neighborhood group called Nextdoor popped up first. She had to enter her address, which made her immediately suspicious, but she could see, just beyond her virtual reach, that people in her zip code were in fact talking about the courts. She could even see her apartment complex listed: Glenvale Terrace. She was desperate to read more, so she reluctantly input the requisite information and began to read her neighbors' takes.

Leonard Nielson
Glenvale Springs Neighborhood

I have lived in Glenvale for coming up on ten years now. It's always been a peaceful, quiet place. But with the addition of these pickleball courts, I can hardly think! It sounds like gunshots all day. What can we do?
17 comments

Lois navigated to the comments and began to read.

Alberta Ramirez
Glenvale Terrace

I have lived in the apartments by the pickleball courts for almost thirty years and the new noise is exhausting. I don't even need an alarm anymore, I'm up when the first ball hits the paddle.

Richard Goode
Glenvale Spring Neighborhood

Yes, gunshots. Exactly. God, could you be any more dramatic? It's not like it's hurting anyone, people are outside and getting exercise. Imagine what it would be like if you lived near a train station.

Leonard Nielson
Glenvale Springs Neighborhood

Trains are intermittent. I even live three blocks away and it is still just nonstop noise.

Leslie Wilson
Glenvale Springs Neighborhood

The city didn't do a noise study before installing the courts. The allowed decibel level is 60-70 DB, but only if players are using a quiet paddle, which many don't, so the independent decibel readings residents have taken range up to 85-90 DB. Additionally, pickleball courts should be 600 ft, at least, from a residence, but these are only 300. The city screwed up.

Brooks Jones
Glenvale Springs Neighborhood

God, this is a bunch of NIMBY garbage! Why is everyone so fragile?

Alberta Ramirez
Glenvale Terrace

You don't even live near the apartments in question.

Resident S.
Glenvale Springs Neighborhood

Why don't you come to downtown out of the suburbs and hear what real gunshots sound like.

Lois was rapt for half an hour reading the comments. She followed those with a linked article about pickleball decibel levels, then continued browsing the rest of the Nextdoor website. She didn't recognize the names of any of her supposed neighbors, which made Lois wonder if she should go to more events at the Senior Center. Most of the posts were about missing pets or items people were trying to give away for free; to Lois it felt like they were saying, "I am too good for this junk, but you might like it."

She eventually abandoned the computer and walked into her kitchen where she made a cup of decaf coffee since she couldn't handle anything with caffeine after noon. Her kitchen window faced the pickleball courts and she could hear a faint pop-pop even with the window closed. She tried not to get irrationally angry about it, it wasn't good for her, but she couldn't help grumbling to herself as she added her sugar-free creamer to the coffee.

How could the city ignore her many petitions? Why wouldn't the landlords help them out? The apartment complex was mostly made up of senior citizens with rent control who had lived there for many years and it felt as if they were entirely invisible. The college students waited on them with impatience while they collected cash from their purses at the grocery stores, dramatically going around them to the self-checkout. And now the internet referred to them as NIMBYs!

She sat back down at the computer and sent another complaint to the city's Noise Department.

To whom it may concern:

I have emailed several times in the past but have only received boilerplate responses. I want to express my disconcertion that nothing has been done at the Glenvale Tennis Courts to deal with the pickleball players who are constantly playing at all hours of the day. The reservation system does not deter them, they get around it. I watched a foursome play with headlamps on just this week!

I am again asking for the city to intervene in some meaningful way as those who are stuck at home either with remote work or disabilities are the most affected. Several of my neighbors have moved out.

I would appreciate a prompt response.
Sincerely, Lois Greene

She pressed send on the email and sipped from her coffee cup, slurping it through her lips, making a sound loud enough to drown out the pop-pop. She wondered if her pleas would make a difference if she were meaner, but Lois found persistence more effective than cruelty. As her mother always told her, "The squeaky wheel gets the grease." Although, so far, the only grease she'd gotten was an automated reply that said: *Thank you for your submission to the Noise Dept., we will answer your letter in the order it was received.*

Lois sighed and decided to go for a walk.

Although she'd retired with a decent pension from the post office, she still missed walking her route every day and tried to get outside as much as possible. She slipped on her shoes with the good inserts and put on a light jacket that she wore almost every day. Her friend, Sharon, had made it for her, sewn it out of an old quilt — it was tacky, and Lois loved it.

As soon as she walked out onto the walking path that separated her apartment complex's parking lot from the tennis and pickleball courts, she saw one of her neighbors exiting his own apartment, gripping a pickleball racket.

Et tu, Brute? She thought to herself.

It wasn't that she minded people having fun or enjoying some exercise, but once a line had been drawn in the sand, she felt it was a betrayal to cross it. Lois stood on the front lines of union pickets for years and possessed an ingrained sense of the unifying power of a group who refused to give in. She'd never play pickleball.

She walked past the courts, the sounds receding behind her, and began her normal circuit. She circled the nearby park where the nannies sat on blankets in a loose circle, letting their young charges lay about in the sun. If the babies tried to crawl away, the nannies simply picked them back up and set them on the blanket again. Never ceasing their chatter to one another, the nannies picked up toys and snacks and doled them out, their hands moving through motions they were already so accustomed to they were hardly motions at all.

In the same park, people threw frisbees and balls to their off-leash dogs. Technically, they were supposed to go to the dog park, but Lois did like dogs, so she never said anything. She paused in her walking to watch a graceful Border Collie jump for a frisbee and return, proud as anything, to his owner. A Labradoodle came galloping into the field with an awkward floppiness that made Lois smile.

Further on, there was a public garden where some of her neighbors spent their time piddling about in raised flower beds. They grew flowers and vegetables and whatever else they thought of, then everything changed over with the arrival of a new season. Lois found it odd that the public garden was locked when no one was in it, she thought that didn't really make it public at all. Lois had never gone inside the garden, but she raised her hand in greeting to a few of the people she recognized, two women in large sunhats and gardening gloves extracting weeds from around tomato plants waved back.

At the back of the park, there was a man who lived in a tent. Lois didn't regularly see him, but she joined the rest of the community in largely ignoring him. If he wasn't hurting anyone, it didn't matter to her that someone camped in the large park. She did wonder now if he was the reason they locked the gate to the public garden. The ladies would certainly not take kindly to someone eating their prized tomatoes, although that's exactly what they were intended for.

Lois turned back toward her apartment. She walked through the subdivision that surrounded the park, houses here went for half a million dollars and up. She felt lucky to be able to live in such a nice place, even if she couldn't afford one of the cottages she'd so envied in her younger years. She'd drop mail off in their boxes or on their porches and think to herself, *one day I'll live in a place just like this, but with blue trim, and sunflowers in the front yard.* Alas, that wish never materialized, but she didn't mind her apartment — what more space did she need, anyway?

On the walk back, she passed the nannies again, one of them picked up a child and, in one swift motion, flipped it over on its stomach. They all laughed about 'tummy time' while Lois strode efficiently past in her comfortable shoes.

She could hear the pickleball courts before she arrived at her apartment. Whatever had unclenched inside of her during the walk tightened again. Then, suddenly, the sound stopped, like when the ocean's tide pulls back against gravity. In the blank silence, she could hear the laughter of the players taking a break, but she also heard something new — a plaintive cry, a mewling, not unlike a baby.

"What on earth," Lois muttered.

In the outdoor breezeway between Lois's door and Chuck's, a small calico cat was sitting daintily on her white socked paws. She launched forward toward Lois when she noticed her approaching and began to rub her head against her leg. Lois's first thought was that she'd get ringworm, or worse, cat hair on her favorite coat. She recoiled, but the cat pursued her.

"Scat!" She cried out, panicked. "Get outta here!"

The cat continued to thread itself around her calves, unperturbed.

She wondered if Chuck had been feeding this little creature, putting out a saucer of milk or tuna fish that she'd begun to rely on for sustenance. He had been gone for a while and Lois considered she might be hungry. Lois didn't know much about cats, she was a dog person, but she knew calico cats were most often female, and she felt a sudden empathy toward the lonely thing.

"Alright, fine."

Lois went to open her door and, as soon as she opened it a crack, the cat squeezed her way inside.

"Hey! Wait a minute!" Lois cried; her keys were still stuck in the lock.

The cat walked confidently to the kitchen, as though she'd been there before, and began to look around. Lois felt herself scrutinized by the feline guest.

"I haven't had time to put the coffee things away," she explained. She hung her coat on the rack by the door and joined the cat in the kitchen.

The cat didn't offer a sound of judgment but sat down again and looked up at Lois.

"Let me see what I have."

Lois dug around in her canned goods cabinet and found an unexpired can of tuna in the back. She didn't know how much cats generally eat, so she dumped it all out onto one of her less used plates.

"Here you go."

The cat dug in greedily and finished the tuna in what felt like only a moment.

"Goodness, you were hungry."

Lois ran the tap and offered her guest a small bowl of water; the cat lowered her head for a few fastidious sips. Then, sated, she wandered off into the living room. Again, Lois felt the cat's gaze.

"It's not much, I know. The furniture really is too big for the space, but I couldn't get rid of it. The sofa is just the right amount of worn in, you know? And I like to put my quilts out, so there's a lot of space for that. I have two more on the bed, but I keep my favorites out here so I can look at them. I don't quilt much anymore; I don't really know why."

The cat, sensing the importance of the quilts, chose a folded one in the corner of the large sectional and carefully climbed on top of it. She made a few biscuits with her tiny paws, then settled down and closed her eyes.

Lois sat on the other end of the sectional, not sure what to do with her hands.

"This is ridiculous, it's my home after all," she said aloud. The cat didn't react.

She turned on the TV and watched a gameshow while the cat slept on. As the sun set and her poorly insulated apartment began to feel the chill of evening, Lois turned on a space heater. The pickleball players had gone home now and everything felt quiet, peaceful. She began to think about what she might make for dinner. She had fresh pasta and an artichoke pesto from the farmer's market, it sounded comforting.

Without her realizing it, the cat had crossed the distance on the sofa separating them and climbed into Lois's lap in search of heat. She hesitatingly stroked the cat's head and was rewarded with a deep-throated purr which stirred something in Lois. They sat together like that until Lois rose to make dinner and put out another half can of tuna for her new friend.

They ate together in the kitchen. Lois read her mystery novels at the table during dinner. It felt indulgent and she liked that. Her own mother would always yell at her for bringing books to the table, but who was going to yell at her now?

The cat licked her paws and sipped at the water, then climbed, uninvited, back onto Lois's lap.

"Hey now," she said, but relented when the cat's small body began to vibrate with purrs and warm her thighs.

"Well, alright," she mumbled, before returning back to her story.

That night the cat, who she had privately begun to refer to as Whiskers, slept at the foot of her bed and Lois situated herself under the cover, being careful not to disturb her sleeping form. She woke once in the night, confused about the weight near her foot, but confusion turned to comfort and she fell back asleep and dreamed of a river she used to visit as a child.

Lois didn't think about checking Nextdoor until the next day. Maybe someone had lost a cat and she'd unwittingly stolen it. She navigated to: *Pets > Lost & Found* and began to click through the posts. No one had posted about a calico cat, so she absolved herself of any guilt and went to make them both breakfast. Lois liked soft scrambled eggs with sour cream and chives most mornings.

The weather was grey and overcast, drizzling intermittently in a way that proffered permission to stay indoors. Whiskers had climbed onto the back of the sofa and was looking outside at the rain as if to say *I can't possibly go out in this.* Lois decided it was not an opportune day to release Whiskers back into the great unknown.

She realized she eventually needed to go to the grocery store and get some proper pet food if this cat was going to become a long-term guest. Also, although Whiskers had so far been polite about it, Lois imagined she'd need a place to go to the bathroom quite soon.

"I guess we'll be roommates for the time being then," Lois said to the cat, who looked back at her in acknowledgment of their arrangement. It felt to Lois like a handshake.

She took her umbrella and walked the two blocks to a small grocery store frequented by other members of her neighborhood. She noticed several people dripping wet, tracking their squeaking wet athletic shoes through the grocery store. They had racket bags strapped to their sides, like they had set out to conquer some great mountain rather than the rubber topped cement of the pickleball courts. They were buying iced coffees and talking too loudly in Lois's opinion.

As Lois was presently on a mission of her own, she felt no animosity, and simply stepped around the pickleball horde to pick up several cans of Fancy Feast, dropping them into her shopping basket and continuing down the aisle. She found kitty litter and a plastic box that was really unacceptable for Whiskers, who she felt deserved something a little nicer to do her business in. *It will do for now*, she thought.

For herself, she collected several jars of her favorite treat, canned peaches, a large box of granola, oat milk, chicken sausages, a prepackaged salad, and some tomatoes. She always did the bulk of her produce shopping at the farmer's market on Sundays, but they, of course, didn't have canned peaches. She imagined eating them out of a bowl with whipped cream and a sprinkle of cinnamon as she breezed through the checkout and past the pickleball players who were still huddled under the awning. Lois deployed her umbrella and walked home with renewed purpose.

Upon opening the door, Whiskers bounded off the sofa and began to rub against her calves. Lois, who wasn't used to being greeted upon arrival, felt comforted by the acknowledgement. She shook out her umbrella and shut the door, though it didn't seem like Whiskers harbored any ideas of escape.

The dim light lent itself to a cozy atmosphere and Lois turned on her space heater.

"Here, I got you a few things. Just so you'll be more comfortable."

She set up the litter box in a corner of her small laundry room and poured a bag of litter in. Whiskers began to meow from behind her, vocalizing her impatience. Lois stepped out of the way and Whiskers hopped into the litter box; Lois went into the kitchen to give the cat some privacy. She prepared both of their snacks and Whiskers greeted her with a mew of relief while they both settled in to dine. Lois read her mystery book at the table, making room for her cat companion when she decided to join her. The rain continued on outside.

Several days passed in the same manner; they became accustomed to one another's schedules and needs. Although they might part ways during the daytime, their evenings were always spent side by side in shared company. Lois did wonder how she might explain Whisker's more or less permanent presence to Chuck when he returned. She hoped he wouldn't be jealous.

When she passed a lost pet poster on her walk, Lois did not scrutinize it too closely. She forgot about checking Nextdoor for postings about missing pets. In fact, she forgot about Nextdoor entirely, and was surprised when she received a notification about the pickleball thread she'd followed so avidly only a few days before. Someone shared a link to an article outlining how the city's Noise Department planned to intervene and install a soundproof barrier along the chain-link fence that enclosed the pickleball court. It was going to cost more than the initial sound study would have cost them and many comments lamented witnessing the ineffectual nature of their 'tax dollars at work.' The Noise Department also sent Lois a follow-up email with a boilerplate template detailing the city's plan. Lois deleted it and then unsubscribed from the Nextdoor aggregate post emails.

Whiskers was sleeping on the couch when Lois turned off her desktop computer and joined her. She stroked the cat's soft belly and watched her little paws flex and her whole body relax into a contented purr. Lois opened an Agatha Christie novel and began to read.

10

Rebecca awoke in her third-floor room, facing the ocean. It was the smallest room in the bed and breakfast retreat she ran on a peninsula in the Gulf Coast. She'd left the windows open overnight and a mosquito had bitten the tender flesh on her shoulder. She scratched at the angry red welt and walked out onto the small balcony. The balcony was the real reason she'd chosen this room as her own; it had just enough space for a chair so she could watch the deep blue waves roll onto the fine beige sand. There were no dunes to obstruct her view. It was a flat expanse all the way to the ocean and she felt as though she stood on the narrow precipice of the entire world.

Her bed and breakfast, appropriately named "The End," was a large beach house with six other bedrooms — a bohemian mélange of doubles, singles and one hostel-style room with several beds. The facade of The End was painted a shade of aquamarine blue that could only belong at the beach. The chef's kitchen was an add-on at the back of the house that led outside to a grill area. Rebecca knew Chris was probably already out there smoking a pork butt. He loved to barbecue and everyone who passed through The End loved him for it.

Today was a turnover day, they only had a couple of guests, but she needed to get the rooms ready for newcomers later in the week. Rebecca dressed in fashionable but functional athleisure and rubber Crocs. She walked downstairs and turned on the coffee pot. Guests were welcome to use the coffee bar in the dining area prior to breakfast if they wanted coffee or some of the pastries that Rebecca purchased from the Polish bakery in town. She made herself a cup of coffee, black, and carried another mug out with her for Chris.

"Morning," she greeted him.

She found him standing over the pit, nudging some of the charcoal. Chris had the look of a washed-up California surfer, but he was raised on a Texas ranch and knew his way around a grill. He wore swim trunks, flip flops, and a band t-shirt, his long hair tied back with a bandana.

"Hey Becky! Mm, thanks for the coffee."

"How long have you been up?"

"Oh, just a couple of hours. I wanted to get the pork butt going and then I thought I might smoke some turkey too, so I had to heat the whole thing up. I want to try these cedar wood chips I got from the guy at the farm stand."

The smoker itself was a homemade monstrosity that Rebecca only tolerated out back and out of sight of the serene spa-like atmosphere she cultivated inside, where everything was ocean green, sky blue, and white. The dark black smoker stayed banished to the backyard.

"There'll be enough meat for the week though."

"I don't know what I'd do without you, Chris."

He looked bashful for a moment, then returned to sopping the meat with a glaze of some kind.

A muggy breeze blew in from the water and fanned her hair back — she felt pleasantly sticky, rolled in salt. When Rebecca had conceptualized The End, she'd imagined it as a place of healing, first and foremost. She deeply identified with the saying: "the cure for anything is salt water — sweat, tears, or the sea." She brought the sea into every aspect of The End's interior space; the decor was understated and natural tones, there were seagrass baskets filled with plush towels, abalone shells used to hold jewelry or keys, and dried pampas grass bouquets in the bedrooms. For the sweat aspect, even though their location on the Gulf Coast made perspiring come easily, Rebecca brought in local yoga instructors three times a week for optional classes. People in the community were invited as well. Of course, the other healing aspect was Chris's food. How could anyone be sad with pulled pork eggs Benedict on the menu?

Rebecca went upstairs to make the beds. Her few guests were all still sleeping, and she liked this quiet time of day where she could let her mind wander as she tucked in hospital corners and replenished the organic, jasmine-scented shampoo and lotion in the bathrooms. She fluffed pillows and hummed to herself contentedly.

Some people didn't understand why she had named her retreat "The End"— why not something more uplifting? But people found The End when they truly needed to escape something more profound than daily struggles. Rebecca had one rule at The End: no cell phones. There was no internet access at all; she had a landline for emergencies, but no Wi-Fi. She asked her guests to entrust her with their cell phones and she kept them in a firesafe lockbox until the visitor felt ready to return to society. Most people handed their phones over willingly, almost thankfully — they were Sisyphus, unburdened of their task, and relief flooded their face knowing they would no longer have to roll the rock uphill.

So, Rebecca had decided, this is the end — a life without the internet, without obligations or intangible attachments, only sensations of the ocean, the occasional mosquitoes, and a return to your own priorities.

Rebecca wanted to ask the question: what would happen if we all just disappeared from the internet? What would social media be without all of us contributing to its endless, hungering maw? A digital Charybdis, sucking us all down beneath the surface. What if one day, we were all just gone? There'd be no one to respond with a fire emoji to your outfit post, no one to fill imaginary squares with intentional FOMO, no one to share a meme in response to a post about something serious.

Rebecca knew better than anyone how it felt to lose yourself in the internet; she had been a meme. A decade prior, her mother held sway as one of the top influencers in the 'Mommy Blogger' culture wars. For years, Rebecca had unknowingly been fodder for her mother's self-aggrandizing stories. Her earliest memory was of her mother saying, "Smile!"

Rebecca never smiled big enough or happily enough for her mother. She was shown other pictures, images of happy little girls wearing flower crowns in a field while their bucolic fashionista mothers wore white dresses reminiscent of Marie Antionette and braided their hair. To Rebecca, those scenes, replayed over and over on her mother's laptop, looked like a tea party she would never be invited to; she sought refuge with her stuffed animals, many of them bearing branded logos, sent by organizations that sponsored her mother's blog.

The edge of competitiveness became more obvious as Rebecca got older. Her mother was always talking about other blogs, how they got more views, more sponsors.

"I want the Disney sponsorship," she complained, showing Rebecca pictures of other women posing at Disney World. "We just have to get the perfect content. Can you try a little harder to smile, sweetheart?"

Rebecca forced smiles at herself in the mirror, while she was brushing her teeth, when no one was looking. She'd put on her cheap dollar store lip gloss and smile, smile, smile.

One of her particularly awkward grimaces, posted on her mother's blog without her consent, became a meme that people used to react in a negative way to things — "cringe-face," someone had described it as. Soon there was a whole *Know Your Meme* page about it. Rebecca's unformed, adolescent features traveled across the internet repeatedly representing people's dislike, someone even re-drew her as a cartoon image which remains popular online. Rebecca came across it once when she still used social media, and her heart wouldn't stop fluttering in her throat. She lay down and thought she was dying until her therapist confirmed she had experienced a panic attack.

Rebecca never saw a dollar of the money her mother made off of her until she turned eighteen. She left her mother alone with her RSS feeds and filed a lawsuit. Eventually, the courts ruled in Rebecca's favor, and she was rewarded some money, enough to buy The End. And now she woke up every morning at an inn facing the ocean and had intentionally created a soft space for the terminally online or unwillingly meme-ed or internet bullied to land. She didn't even have to advertise; visitors came to her primarily by word of mouth — those who wanted a place to truly unplug or possibly disappear knew The End was the place to do it.

Rebecca hadn't spoken to her mother in years, but knew she sold essential oils online now — she'd watched a video of her aging mother putting drops of rosemary oil on her scalp, drops of peppermint oil in her tea, looking desperate.

She ceased her wandering thoughts and focused on her remaining tasks for the day.

Right now, she had two people staying with her. The first guy, Chuck, had been here for a couple of weeks now. She recognized the familiar relief in his bloodshot eyes when he'd handed over his phone, and he hadn't once asked for it back. The first night, she heard him pacing the bedroom until dawn. After the first couple of days, he started coming downstairs and chatting with Chris, then took himself for a long run down the beach and came back to eat breakfast.

She heard his door open and poked her head down the hallway.

"Good morning, Chuck."

"Hey Rebecca! I'm just gonna go for a run, but I smell Chris smoking something."

"He's got a pork butt *and* a turkey going this morning. It won't be ready until brunch though. I can whip you up some eggs in the meantime if you'd like."

"Yeah," he smiled at her, his whole face lighting up like a child's. "Yeah, that would be great. Thanks."

She watched him carry his running shoes downstairs.

Rebecca's other guest hadn't left her room since arriving and, now that she'd finished getting the turnover rooms ready, she knocked on the door to check in.

"Yes?" Came a timid reply.

"Hey, I just wanted to make sure you were feeling okay. Do you need anything?"

"I... I think I'm going to come downstairs."

"Okay, whatever you'd like. There's coffee, tea, and pastries. I can also make eggs any way you like them."

The woman opened the door. She had chipped black nail polish and long hair; her makeup was smudged around her eyes as though she hadn't washed her face in a day or two.

Rebecca remembered her audible sigh of relief when she'd handed over her phone.

"I like scrambled eggs, if that's possible."

"Of course!"

Rebecca carried an armload of towels downstairs with her and threw them into the wash. Then, she headed into the kitchen. She made eggs like Julia Child, with loads of cream and butter and a dusting of thinly sliced chives.

She overheard Chris and Chuck talking through the open kitchen window, the smell of smoked meat permeating the air.

"You know, I watched you win a *Trash Fighters* tournament on Twitch once."

"Yeah? You're allowed to watch Twitch?"

They both laughed and Rebecca smiled too.

"Yeah, I didn't want to tell you at first. I know everyone comes here for their own reasons; they don't necessarily like to be reminded of why."

"I came here because I needed to sleep. I was under so much pressure from everyone — the other players, the tournament organizers, my sponsor, and more than anything, the fans. They wanted a piece of me so badly, expected things of me, I just couldn't handle it."

"I can't imagine what that's like."

"And it's weird, like, I could go to Walmart, and no one would know who I was at all, I just bought peanut butter and left. But if I went to anything gaming adjacent it was just such a sharp turn. There was so much pressure, and if I *did* lose, people were so disappointed in me. It made me feel like a little kid, always letting everyone down."

Rebecca's heart went out to him in that moment, she thought of herself smiling endlessly into the camera her mother shoved in her face. Their conversation was muffled now, and Rebecca expertly flipped the eggs onto a plate.

When she emerged from the kitchen, the woman from upstairs was chewing on her thumbnail in the dining area, looking lost.

"You can sit at one of the tables or eat on the deck if you'd prefer."

She obediently took the nearest seat.

"Here are your eggs. Would you like a coffee?"

"Yes. Do you have oat milk?"

"Sure, let me grab it out of the fridge."

While she made the coffee, Rebecca noticed the woman ate with gusto and felt relieved that she had an appetite. She tried to remember her name; it was something unique. Rebecca snuck a quick peak at her reservation book. *Astrid, oh yeah*, she thought triumphantly.

"Here you go, Astrid," she addressed her, handing off the coffee.

"Thanks."

Rebecca could sense when her guests didn't want to talk, so she went back to the kitchen to assess what items might need restocking on her next trip back to the mainland. She watched Astrid rise, her long skirt skimming the ground, she'd paired it with a crop top and Rebecca thought admiringly that she looked like a witch on vacation.

Astrid's long fingers skimmed the trading post library Rebecca cultivated in the lounge area, its signage encouraged guests to take or leave a book. At one point, the library was eighty percent some influencer named Anthem's manifestation journal, and Rebecca had to constantly cull the millennial pink self-help planner from the stacks. The lounge itself contained two pairs of mismatched recliners, a small end table between each, and a long chaise lounge under the window. She'd filled the room with sun catchers, stained glass, and hanging plants so it felt both open and cozy. It also distracted from the fact that there wasn't a television or computer in sight.

One guest, a young woman named Kassie, had complained vocally for days about the lack of television.

"I just don't know what to *do*," she had whined to Rebecca.

Rebecca, who understood her plight, could hardly believe Kassie was *so* famous online that she'd needed to come to The End in hiding; multiple wigs were employed during her stay.

"Take a walk by the ocean."

"It's so boring."

"How can you be bored of the ocean?"

"How can you not?"

Eventually, she had gone for a walk and stopped complaining and, Rebecca strongly suspected, had a brief fling with Chris before leaving.

Weeks later, Kassie sent a postcard of a rainbow over a pristine beach emblazoned with a hot pink graphic that said: "Maui Wowie!" In it, she expressed a brief thank you to Rebecca and acknowledged: *You were right, how can anyone get bored of the ocean?*

Rebecca privately considered Kassie one of her success stories.

Astrid selected a book and sat down on the chaise lounge to thumb through it and drink her coffee. Rebecca nodded to herself, at the very least she was glad Astrid had moved out of her room and into the common area where she might get a little sun and social interaction. It seemed like a big step.

"Whew! It's getting crispy!" Chris called from out back. "It might be more of a sunset pork butt than a brunch one though."

Rebecca rolled her eyes and walked out onto the elevated first floor deck; the whole house was raised up on wooden stilts due to the constant threat of hurricanes. From her perch, she could see Chuck running down the beach. She watched him slow down, raise his arms over his head and turn to face the waves. He stood there for quite a while, unmoving, then Rebecca watched as he removed his shoes and stepped into the water, splashing out in an uncoordinated manner she could only describe as 'free.'

He walked back toward the house, damp, his hair tousled. Rebecca noted that he'd gotten quite a tan since arriving, his pale indoor skin was bronze and resplendent with vitamin D. He walked around back to first talk to Chris, she turned from the kitchen just in time to see

Astrid and Chuck clock each other in the lounge area. Chuck hesitated, then walked toward her and said something. Astrid smiled at him, and Rebecca watched their conversation, silent for her, through the windowpane.

She waited a decent amount of time, then walked in and announced, "Chris's butt won't be ready until this evening."

Both of her guests turned, eyes wide.

"The pork butt, I meant!"

They all laughed.

"Well, I was thinking I might set up the fire pit down on the beach tonight, even though it's going to be warm."

"That sounds great!" Chuck agreed enthusiastically.

Astrid nodded; she'd placed her book open on her knee.

Chuck went upstairs and Astrid made another cup of coffee, then tucked her feet up under her thighs and continued reading. Rebecca tidied the kitchen and called in her order to the grocery store for pick up the following day. She wasn't expecting any new guests until Friday, so she only had Chuck and Astrid and herself to feed until then. To be fair though, Chuck ate a lot. The rest of the morning passed languidly.

In the late afternoon, a car pulled into their long driveway.

"Becky!" Chris called from the back porch where he had begun to wind down from a day of meat smoking with a beer.

Rebecca poked her head outside.

"What?"

"Are you expecting anyone?"

"Not today."

They lived too far down the peninsula for any guests to be accidental and Rebecca immediately panicked that there was some sort of emergency or that a guest had geotagged them online, something she directly discouraged. The last thing she needed was to become a viral retreat for virtual stars with trust fund money.

A giant of a man in gym shorts and flip flops climbed out of the driver's side of the truck now parked in the driveway; he walked to the passenger door and helped out a woman with electric purple hair and chunky platform sandals that still barely brought her up to the guy's shoulders.

"Can we help you?" Rebecca called out from the porch, crossing her arms in a protective mama bear stance.

"Uh, yeah, I... uh," the guy faltered and ran his hand nervously through his hair.

"I'm Molly, this is Brian."

"And what do y'all want?"

"We're looking for Chuck."

"Who's that?" Rebecca bluffed.

"He's a gamer, we think he may have come here. It's just, well, people are really worried about him."

"There are theories on Reddit that he *died*," Brian burst out. "People are planning his virtual funeral. And his old lady neighbor stole his cat!"

Rebecca didn't try to further decipher the situation.

"Y'all stay here. Chris, watch them."

Chris nodded and the newcomers shifted back and forth on their feet while Rebecca ran upstairs. She knocked softly on Chuck's door; he opened it still wearing his swim trunks and a confused expression.

"Hey?"

"This is going to sound strange, but there's a certain Brian and Molly downstairs looking for you and I didn't tell them you were here, but they seem to think it's awfully important that they see you."

"Brian?"

Rebecca pointed to his window and Chuck peered out.

"Oh shit, that's Porky."

Rebecca shrugged.

"I don't know who the girl is. Did Porky finally get laid? Oh man, this is great."

"So, do you want to see them?"

Chuck hesitated and bit his bottom lip, chapped from the sun.

"Yeah, I do. Should I go downstairs, or are they allowed in? I don't know how it works."

"You can have visitors, it's not a prison."

Chuck smiled, "Alright. Give me five minutes and I'll come down."

Rebecca walked back downstairs and called over the railing, "Chuck's coming down."

"Oh shit," Brian muttered. "He's actually here."

Molly patted his hand and smiled up at him, her hair glistening in the sun like a lilac just emerged from the snow.

"Would either of y'all like a beer?"

"Yes!" Brian cried.

"Come on up."

They climbed the short flight of stairs to stand with Rebecca and Chris on the elevated porch. Rebecca smiled at them and pulled two bottles out of the porch mini fridge. They followed her along the wooden wraparound porch to where The End had the best view of the ocean. Chris settled back in his Adirondack chair, and Rebecca thought Brian seemed less awkward now that he had something to do with his hands.

"So, how long have you had this place?" Molly asked.

"It's been a few years now. I run it mostly by myself, Chris helps."

Chris raised his beer in acknowledgement.

"How did you find us?" Rebecca asked.

"Word of mouth, people were not keen to give up the location and we had to express the urgency."

"It *is* peaceful here," Brian added.

It was then Chuck finally descended the stairs and joined them.

Brian looked genuinely shocked to see him.

"What the fuck, man?"

Chuck just laughed and gave the large man a hug. "Did you miss getting your ass kicked by me *that* much?"

"Dude, people think you're dead!"

"Nah, just happy."

Rebecca motioned with her head for Chris to follow her inside. He nodded, the pork butt was done, the turkey had been retrieved earlier. They sat in the kitchen together and Rebecca poured herself a glass of white wine from an uncorked bottle in the fridge.

"So, I know you know, what's the story?" Rebecca asked her friend.

Chris gave her a quick rundown of numbChux's disappearance right before a major tournament his sponsor had helped organize, how the internet had gone wild with conspiracy theories, as they are wont to do. He even knew about PorkyDig losing to DramaLlama, who was also his new girlfriend, Molly.

Rebecca shook her head. It was wild to think that the internet was still out there, existing, without her taking any active part in it. The whirlpool went on without her, she could not reject it wholly.

The sun began to set and Rebecca gathered up the meat, potato salad, corn and booze and loaded it into a cooler. Chris carried it down to the beach and she informed Astrid they had guests and did she want to come down to the beach?

"Sure, let me get some bug spray first."

"Good idea," Rebecca acknowledged.

She called out to the newly assembled group of gamers, "Do y'all want to come down to the beach for food and fire?"

"Hell yeah," Chuck cried.

Brian looked somewhat taken aback, but they all dutifully followed Rebecca down to the sandy pit Chris had dug out and filled with dry wood. The evening felt heavy with moisture, but soon the fire was crackling, sending sparks up into the sky. They watched the sun sink into the ocean in silence.

Rebecca passed out food, beer, and poured wine for herself and Astrid. The first few moments were awkward, as at any dinner party, but soon her four charges were talking amongst themselves. Molly, it turned out, recognized Astrid from YouTube and, at first, Astrid seemed uncomfortable, but soon they were talking and even laughing about the wild comments women get from simply existing online. Brian and Chuck were engaged in a deep, private discussion, their heads bent close together.

Rebecca joined Chris on a washed-up log they often sat on and stared at the flames licking upward toward the sky. She felt proud in that moment, proud that she could bring people some semblance of peace or acceptance or community.

Chris smiled at her, his face half lit by the flame, the other half in shadows. *Yes, my unconventional found family*, Rebecca thought to herself.

Brian and Molly ended up staying the night, which turned into a week. They agreed to lock up their phones up alongside Chuck's and, with Astrid, became a cozy foursome that played chess together in the evening. Brian and Molly were both wildly competitive and the games escalated into crowing taunts before the evening's end.

When the time came for everyone to leave, Rebecca felt a pang, as though she were losing her own adult children. As they each bid her and Chris goodbye, with promises to visit again soon, she released their phones back to them and politely ignored Chuck and Astrid holding hands as they left and sent them silent well wishes for whatever came next.

She sighed and Chris shrugged, then walked back out to his barbecue outpost; he was smoking a brisket today. Her next visitors were coming that afternoon and Rebecca still had to tidy the rooms. They were hosting a community yin yoga class that evening, she needed to restock white wine and pick up fresh pastries, then she hoped to take a walk along the beach with Chris that evening — there was so much to do.

Is it the End of the Internet as We Know it?

With more streamers taking leaves of absence and fewer teens reporting aspirations to be YouTube stars, is it the end of the golden age of streaming?

<u>Click to read more></u>

ABOUT THE AUTHOR

Abigail Stewart is a fiction writer from the California desert. She is the author of three previous books, *The Drowned Woman*, *Assemblage*, and *Foundations*. Find her at helloabigailstewart.com

ABOUT THE PUBLISHER

Whisk(e)y Tit is committed to restoring degradation and degeneracy to the literary arts. We work with authors who are unwilling to sacrifice intellectual rigor, unrelenting playfulness, and visual beauty in our literary pursuits, often leading to texts that would otherwise be abandoned in today's largely homogenized literary landscape. In a world governed by idiocy, our commitment to these principles is an act of civil service and civil disobedience alike.

www.ingramcontent.com/pod-product-compliance
Lightning Source LLC
Chambersburg PA
CBHW070513200726
48293CB00007B/2510